We Believe

We Believe

30 Days to Understanding Our Heritage

Jack Watts and David Dunham

DUNHAM
BOOKS

The authors wish to point out that the documents that are cited and/or replicated in this book have not been altered from their original form. There are several differences in the spelling of certain words between the British and American and there are several instances where the author of the letter or document actually misspelled certain words— e.g. Paul Revere spelling "chiefly" as "cheifly," and "intelligence" as "intelegence."

Printed in the United States of America
ISBN 978-1-4507-3578-0

Book design and layout by Darlene Swanson • www.van-garde.com

Dedication

For our children, our grandchildren,
our great-grandchildren, and beyond—
that they would continue to experience the
freedoms and blessings bestowed upon
our generation by the patriots who created
our great American heritage.

Contents

Preface

We believe that America is indeed the land of the free and the home of the brave. Throughout our perilous history, we have faced many obstacles and weathered many storms. We may survive many more, but we cannot do so without being vigilant—without being informed. With perils from without and from within, understanding core American values is more important than ever.

Our goal is to help our fellow Americans recognize our extraordinary heritage so that they can embrace our belief system more firmly than ever. That's why we have created *We Believe: 30 days to Understanding Our Heritage*.

It's our hope that by reading *We Believe* you will become a citizen who understands our shared history and is willing to make a stand for the values we hold so dear. We encourage you to take the 30-day challenge, which will help make you a better-informed American.

We are not alone in our goal. Others have been instrumental in making *We Believe* a powerful and inspirational educational tool. Aiding us in our endeavor, Emily Prather's assistance has been invaluable. Her editorial and organizational skills have made *We Believe* an extraordinary resource. Mark Horne, a noted author and historian added valuable material to the book. Darlene Swanson's layout has made *We Believe* easy to read and understand. Finally, Dwayne Bassett's cover beautifully depicts the values we hold dear.

To each, we say thank you.

Jack Watts
Atlanta, Georgia

David Dunham
Nashville, Tennessee

Introduction

Recently, while walking around the indoor track at the YMCA, a young man, who had been jogging, finished his run and cooled down by walking beside me. As we started to chat, I pointed out a much older man ahead of us who was walking quite slowly. I said to the jogger, "Do you see that man in front of us?"

Looking ahead, he replied, "Yeah."

"He fought in the Battle of the Bulge," I said, in an obvious effort to pay tribute to one of the few remaining heroes of World War II.

Without missing a beat, the young man responded, "How much did he lose?"

Instantly aware that my young acquaintance had no idea what the Battle of the Bulge was, believing the older man had been a TV-show contestant, I replied, "Quite a bit." I didn't want to embarrass the jogger, so I played along and eventually changed the subject.

As I thought about the incident later, the humorous aspects started to trouble me. I became quite concerned about how Americans—especially younger ones—have lost their sense of history. My experience had a surreal quality, as if it was a light-hearted moment which revealed a deep-seated problem in our culture. It became crystal clear to me that there are millions of Americans drifting through life unaware of what we, as a nation, believe—unaware of what America is all about.

As the days passed, my sense of concern increased, and I began to wonder how this problem could be remedied. A few weeks later, while I was in Nashville, I had a cup of coffee with a friend of nearly three decades, David Dunham. Relating the story to him, we began a serious dialog about the huge gap in understanding which exists among many people about what our forefathers believed and about our rich historical tradition.

Concurring, our conversation turned to how dangerous it is for our republic to have citizens who have such limited awareness of the core values upon which our nation was established. Having published at least twenty-five *New York Times* bestsellers—several in the history and political genres—David turned the conversation to specific ways in which we might be able to make a positive impact upon those who want to increase their awareness of our country's rich heritage based on our Constitution as well as other significant documents over the past 200-plus years.

From that initial meeting, we developed a plan to publish *We Believe: 30 Days to Understanding Our Heritage.* Our goal was to provide a quick, easy way for interested people to learn what our Founding Fathers believed, coupled with what others have added in subsequent generations—all of which has added texture and value to the Founders' ideas.

As we developed our concept, we made a deliberate, conscientious commitment to abstain from any partisan editorial comments about the documents. We believed that editorializing would detract from their power and integrity. In our commitment to fairness and accuracy, we have included numerous excerpts from both Democrat and Republican leaders. Our goal, which we have maintained scrupulously, is to allow the voices of our great leaders to speak for themselves, enhanced only by our efforts to couch them within their historical perspective.

This short book, which is packed with the core values of our heritage, can be read quickly and easily. By taking ten minutes a day for thirty days, anybody can come to understand the values upon which America was founded. Every reader will learn why these values are critical to our future and why the generations that preceded us have fought so fiercely to preserve them, often spilling their blood to do so.

In the twenty-first century, the United States faces new challenges and new dangers, which once again require an informed citizenry to make a stand for what we have always believed. To remain strong, we must remain resolute. To remain resolute, we must have convictions. To have convictions, we must know what we believe. To know what we believe, we must return to the original documents. There is no other way.

In the nineteenth century, Lord Acton pointed out, "The only thing necessary for evil to triumph is for good men to do nothing." His words seem more appropriate today than when he first spoke them. We live in perilous times—times which require good men and women to stand firmly against those who hate our way of life and who plot to destroy it. We also face dangers from within—from those who are Americans but who no longer embrace our core values as their own. There have always been people like this among us; but their numbers have grown so large today, they threaten to overwhelm those of us who embrace our heritage lovingly, willingly, and reverently.

For decades, I've heard people warn of impending doom; and like most, I've dismissed what they have had to say as nonsense—as ludicrous, conspiratorial rhetoric. Now, their warnings of impending disaster don't seem as farfetched as they once did. As most

Americans are coming to realize, being ignorant about our heritage is no longer an option.

Remaining unaware may have a heavy price tag attached. For example, in Holland, before World War II, there were 120,000 Jews. By the end of the war, more than 100,000 of them had been exterminated. As one young Jewish girl wrote:

On the last day of school, I failed geography.
A week later I found out exactly where Treblinka was.
But only for a week.

America has weathered many storms. We may weather many more, but we cannot do so without being vigilant—without being informed. With perils from without and from within, understanding our great tradition is more important than ever. Keeping that in mind, we have created *We Believe: 30 days to Understanding Your Heritage*, which we are certain will help our fellow Americans become a better-informed electorate.

Jack Watts
Atlanta, Georgia

1

Give me liberty, or give me death!
—Patrick Henry

On March 23, 1775, at St. John's Church in Richmond, Virginia, Patrick Henry delivered a speech that is credited with having convinced the Virginia House of Burgesses to pass a resolution committing the Virginia troops to the Revolutionary War. Among those in attendance were Thomas Jefferson and George Washington. So stirring was the speech that William Wirt wrote:

> No murmur of applause was heard. The effect was too deep. After the trance of a moment, several members started from their seats. The cry, 'to arms,' seemed to quiver on every lip, and gleam from every eye! . . . That supernatural voice still sounded in their ears, and shivered along their arteries. . . . They became impatient of speech—their souls were on fire for action. (p. 123, *Life and Character of Patrick Henry*, by William Wirt, 1816)

"Give Me Liberty or Give Me Death,"
by Patrick Henry, March 23, 1775

Mr. President, it is natural to man to indulge in the illusions of hope. We are apt to shut our eyes against a painful truth, and listen to the song of that siren till she transforms us into beasts. Is this the part of wise men, engaged in a great and arduous struggle for liberty? Are we disposed to be of the numbers of those who, having eyes, see not, and, having ears, hear not, the things which so nearly concern their temporal salvation?

As human beings, we have a strong impulse toward denial. We would rather believe a situation is not that bad rather than admit a painful reality. People tend to assume that if they do nothing, the people with power—those in charge—will recover their senses and act appropriately. Patrick Henry understood that there was no reason to believe that Britain was going to begin acting reasonably. The colonies had tried everything they could to peaceably make known their petition for representation in the British Parliament. Instead of listening to the people, however, the British government responded by sending troops to quell the colonial unrest.

To persuade his audience, Henry used well-known literary references. First, he invoked *The Odyssey*—the story of Odysseus and his legendary voyage to Greece. According to the poet, Homer, the sirens were creatures with the bodies of huge birds and the chest and heads of human women. They would sing from the land, and their song would drive sailors so mad they would turn their ships toward the source of the song. But there were dangerous reefs in the way. When the ships broke upon the rocks, the sirens would fly to the drowning sailors, pick them from the water, and devour them.

The second story Patrick Henry used is found in the Bible. The prophet Jeremiah said, "Hear now this, O foolish people, and without understanding; which have eyes, and see not; which have ears, and hear not" (Jeremiah 5:21; see also Ezekiel 12:2, KJV). Christ also spoke these words: "Having eyes, see ye not? And having ears, hear ye not? And do ye not remember?" (Mark 8:18, KJV).

By appealing to his audience's common heritage, Patrick Henry was able to drive home the danger of the colonists denying reality at a time when the British government was about to invade and occupy the land.

Sir, we have done everything that could be done to avert the storm which is now coming on. We have petitioned; we have remonstrated; we have supplicated; we have prostrated ourselves before the throne, and have implored its interposition to arrest the tyrannical hands of the ministry and Parliament. Our petitions have been slighted; our remonstrances have produced additional violence and insult; our supplications have been disregarded; and we have been spurned, with contempt, from the foot of the throne! In vain, after these things, may we indulge the fond hope of peace and reconciliation.

The source of the taxation problems for the colonies didn't come from King George—it came from the British Parliament. As Englishmen, with the traditional rights of Englishmen, the colonists were outraged that a legislative body was claiming ownership of them—even though they had no representation in that body. So, the colonists had appealed to the king for protection. Unfortunately, the king sided with Parliament rather than with the colonists and traditional English law.

> If we wish to be free—if we mean to preserve inviolate those inestimable privileges for which we have been so long contending—if we mean not basely to abandon the noble struggle in which we have been so long engaged, and which we have pledged ourselves never to abandon until the glorious object of our contest shall be obtained—we must fight!

The colonies were unwilling to be ruled and taxed by a legislative body that did not allow them to have elected representation. Presenting a clear choice, Henry argued that, unless they took the step of armed resistance, the colonists would be giving up their rights.

> The millions of people, armed in the holy cause of liberty, and in such a country as that which we possess, are invincible by any force which our enemy can send against us. Besides, sir, we shall not fight our battles alone. There is a just God who presides over the destinies of nations, and who will raise up friends to fight our battles for us. The battle, sir, is not to the strong alone; it is to the vigilant, the active, the brave. Besides, sir, we have no election. If we were base enough to desire it, it is now too late to retire from the contest. There is no retreat but in submission and slavery! Our chains are forged! Their clanking may be heard on the plains of Boston! The war is inevitable—and let it come! I repeat it, sir, let it come.

This paragraph contains a series of separate, short arguments:

1.   The colonists were strong enough to fight Britain.

3424

2. God was on their side and would help them.

3. God would make certain they had allies. There were other nations that would take their side, including France.

4. The limited military resources of the colonies were a problem, but there were positive factors as well. Immediate and decisive leadership was even more important, which necessitated quick and brave action.

5. Avoiding conflict was *not* an option; rather, the choice was to resist or to surrender to military domination.

It is in vain, sir, to extenuate the matter. Gentlemen may cry, Peace, Peace—but there is no peace. The war is actually begun! The next gale that sweeps from the north will bring to our ears the clash of resounding arms! Our brethren are already in the field! Why stand we here idle? What is it that gentlemen wish? What would they have? Is life so dear, or peace so sweet, as to be purchased at the price of chains and slavery? Forbid it, Almighty God! I know not what course others may take; but as for me, give me liberty or give me death!

Henry wanted his audience to stop deluding themselves into thinking they could trust Parliament to restore their rights. He said that it would be better for them to die fighting for freedom than to live as slaves to England.

2

O say, does that star-spangled banner
yet wave; O'er the land of the free
and the home of the brave?
—FRANCIS SCOTT KEY

On September 13-14, 1814, Francis Scott Key witnessed the bombardment of American forces by the British Royal Navy. It was in the Battle of Baltimore during the War of 1812. Key, a young American attorney, was at sea those two days and could not tell the result of the battle until the morning. He was certain the sheer ferocity of the British assault did not portend a hopeful outcome. At dawn, however, Key was enthused as he saw the large American flag flying triumphantly above Fort McHenry. Inspired, he wrote the poem, *Defence of Fort McHenry*, from which the lyrics for "The Star-Spangled Banner" come.

On March 3, 1931, "The Star-Spangled Banner" was declared the national anthem by a congressional resolution, which was signed by President Herbert Hoover.

The Star-Spangled Banner, 1814

Oh, say can you see, by the dawn's early light,
What so proudly we hailed at the twilight's last gleaming?
Whose broad stripes and bright stars, through the perilous fight,
O'er the ramparts we watched, were so gallantly streaming?
And the rockets' red glare, the bombs bursting in air,
Gave proof through the night that our flag was still there.
O say, does that star-spangled banner yet wave
O'er the land of the free and the home of the brave?

The first stanza is the most famous and is usually the only stanza sung when "The Star-Spangled Banner" is performed. The rockets Francis Scott Key wrote about were some of the earliest self-propelled missiles used in war. They were called Congreve rockets after Sir William Congreve, who invented them. Congreve took the biggest skyrockets he could find in London and transformed them into self-propelled missiles. The British Army and Navy used them from about 1806 to 1815 when improvements in other weapons made Congreve rockets obsolete.

On the shore, dimly seen through the mists of the deep,
Where the foe's haughty host in dread silence reposes,
What is that which the breeze, o'er the towering steep,
As it fitfully blows, now conceals, now discloses?
Now it catches the gleam of the morning's first beam,
In full glory reflected now shines on the stream:
'Tis the star-spangled banner! O long may it wave
O'er the land of the free and the home of the brave.

The sheer ferocity of the British bombardment didn't give Key much to hope for that fateful night, as he anxiously awaited the outcome of the battle. After all, the British Navy was the most feared in the world. Imagine Key's joy when he saw the American flag raised high above Fort McHenry. He captured his jubilation, immortalizing his feeling with the words, "In full glory now shines on the stream: 'tis the star-spangled banner!" signifying the Americans had triumphed.

And where is that band who so vauntingly swore
That the havoc of war and the battle's confusion
A home and a country should leave us no more?
Their blood has wiped out their foul footstep's pollution.
No refuge could save the hireling and slave
From the terror of flight, or the gloom of the grave:
And the star-spangled banner in triumph doth wave
O'er the land of the free and the home of the brave.

In the War of 1812, the British faced a second defeat against the upstart Americans. Though America had won its independence in the Revolutionary War just a few decades earlier, the British believed the nascent country wouldn't survive the War of 1812. But, as Key so accurately wrote, "the star-spangled banner in triumph doth wave; o'er the land of the free, and the home of the brave."

Oh! thus be it ever, when freemen shall stand
Between their loved homes and the war's desolation!
Blest with victory and peace, may the heaven-rescued land
Praise the Power that hath made and preserved us a nation.

Then conquer we must, for our cause it is just,
And this be our motto: "In God is our trust."
And the star-spangled banner forever shall wave
O'er the land of the free and the home of the brave!

From this verse comes the motto of the United States, "In God we trust." In 1956, the United States adopted this slogan as the national motto and made it law. Key ended his poem as he ended each preceding stanza, with the patriotic description of America as "the land of the free and the home of the brave!" Certainly the soldiers in the fight Key had witnessed had proven this to be true.

3

We hold these Truths to be self-evident, that all Men are created equal, that they are endowed by their Creator with unalienable Rights, that among these are Life, Liberty and the Pursuit of Happiness.

—THE DECLARATION OF INDEPENDENCE

The Declaration of Independence, written primarily by Thomas Jefferson, was adopted by the Continental Congress on July 4, 1776. The document is the formal explanation of why the Continental Congress voted on July 2 to declare independence from Great Britain, more than a year after the start of the Revolutionary War.

July 4—Independence Day—is celebrated annually as the birthday of America.

The Declaration of Independence, July 4, 1776

We hold these Truths to be self-evident, that all Men are created equal, that they are endowed by their Creator with certain unalienable Rights, that among these are Life, Liberty and the Pursuit of Happiness – That to secure these Rights,

> Governments are instituted among Men, deriving their just Powers from the Consent of the Governed, that whenever any Form of Government becomes destructive to these Ends, it is the Right of the People to alter or to abolish it, and to institute new Government, laying its Foundation on such Principles and organizing its Powers in such Form, as to them shall seem most likely to effect their Safety and Happiness. Prudence, indeed, will dictate that Governments long established should not be changed for light and transient Causes; and accordingly all Experience hath shown that Mankind are more disposed to suffer, while Evils are sufferable, than to right themselves by abolishing the Forms to which they are accustomed. But when a long Train of Abuses and Usurpations, pursuing invariably the same Object, evinces a Design to reduce them under absolute Despotism, it is their Right, it is their Duty, to throw off such Government, and to provide new Guards for their future Security.

Although the preamble is not a legal document, it powerfully encompasses the core values of the American dream. In these few short words, the American vision was created and shaped by Thomas Jefferson.

The Declaration assumes that all governments are based on the consent of the people. Even a dictatorship requires a great deal of cooperation from the people, or it could not exist. People often tolerate poor governments because "prudence" makes clear that revolutions are dangerous and can result in even worse forms of government. Recognizing the "long train of abuses" coming from Parliament and the king, the rebellious colonists believed they had an opportunity, which was "their right" and "their duty" to pursue—to form a new and better government.

HE has called together Legislative Bodies at Places unusual, uncomfortable, and distant from the Depository of their public Records, for the sole Purpose of fatiguing them into Compliance with his Measures.

The "He" here refers to King George, who was the primary focus of the Declaration. In fact, most of the document is a list of the abuses inflicted on the colonies by the king. This is just one example. A government can provide formal justice while inflicting injustice. In this case, English-appointed colonial governors in Massachusetts and Virginia moved the location of legislative assemblies on the grounds of security, but they really intended to discourage colonial activists from objecting to new laws.

HE has erected a Multitude of new Offices, and sent hither Swarms of Officers to harass our People, and eat out their Substance.

The British government sent their customs officers to America, while imposing the burden of military courts on the established colonial court system. There also were additional financial burdens placed on the colonists, for which they never voted. While native Englishmen addressed such issues through their representatives in Parliament, the colonists had to submit to these new laws with no opportunity for redress.

HE has combined with others to subject us to a Jurisdiction foreign to our Constitution, and unacknowledged by our Laws; giving his Assent to their Acts of pretended Legislation:

This complaint is the basic argument in the Declaration. The colonists understood they were the subjects of the king—just like Englishmen in their native land were subjects of the king. Just as those Englishmen had a legislative body called Parliament, so each of the thirteen colonies had a legislative body made up of elected representatives. Parliament, however, claimed the right to pass laws impacting the colonists—laws the colonists thought were illegal. The colonists believed it was illegal for the king to assert that Parliament had such power over them.

★   ★   ★

IN every stage of these Oppressions we have Petitioned for Redress in the most humble Terms: Our repeated Petitions have been answered only by repeated Injury. A Prince, whose Character is thus marked by every act which may define a Tyrant, is unfit to be the Ruler of a free People.

NOR have we been wanting in Attentions to our British Brethren. We have warned them from Time to Time of attempts by their Legislature to extend an unwarrantable Jurisdiction over us. We have reminded them of the Circumstances of our Emigration and Settlement here. We have appealed to their native Justice and Magnanimity, and we have conjured them by the Ties of our common Kindred to disavow these Usurpations, which, would inevitably

interrupt our Connections and Correspondence. They too have been deaf to the Voice of Justice and Consanguinity.

The colonies tried every way they knew to get King George and Parliament to stop their actions—which the colonists considered to be illegal. The colonists also tried to gain enough sympathy with the English public to influence Parliament to stop abusing the colonies. Notice that the assumption of the Declaration is not that the American colonists want to *become* "a free People." Rather, it is that they *are already* free, which is a big difference.

WE, therefore, the Representatives of the UNITED STATES of AMERICA, in General Congress, Assembled, appealing to the Supreme Judge of the World for the Rectitude of our Intentions, do, in the Name, and by the Authority of the good People of these Colonies, solemnly Publish and Declare, that these United Colonies are, and of Right ought to be, FREE AND INDEPENDENT STATES; that they are absolved from all Allegiance to the British Crown, and that all political Connection between them and the State of Great Britain, is and ought to be totally dissolved; and that as FREE AND INDEPENDENT STATES, they have full Power to levy War, conclude Peace, contract Alliances, establish Commerce, and to do all other Acts and Things which INDEPENDENT STATES may of right do. And for the support of this Declaration, with a firm Reliance on the Protection of Divine Providence, we mutually pledge to each other our Lives, our Fortunes, and our sacred Honor.

With this statement, American history was changed forever. The colonies publicly proclaimed independence from England; there was no turning back. The term "United States of America" should not be confused with the nation founded later under the Constitution. The Declaration does not enact the existence of a single nation but rather thirteen "free and independent states"—each with full power to act as a nation. Later, these states voluntarily consented to form a single nation under the Constitution—the United States of America.

4

> *And so, my fellow Americans: ask not what*
> *your country can do for you—ask what you*
> *can do for your country.*
> —JOHN F. KENNEDY

John F. Kennedy was America's 35th president. Elected in 1960, President Kennedy served until his assassination on November 22, 1963. As is the long-standing tradition for U.S. presidents, he delivered his inaugural address shortly after taking the presidential oath of office. Although among the shortest inaugural addresses in U.S. history, Kennedy's speech is widely considered to be one of the best.

President John F. Kennedy's
Inaugural Address, January 20, 1961

The world is very different now. For man holds in his mortal hands the power to abolish all forms of human poverty and all forms of human life. And yet the same revolutionary beliefs for which our forebears fought are still at issue around the globe–the belief that the rights of man come not from the generosity of the state but from the hand of God.

We dare not forget today that we are the heirs of that first revolution. Let the word go forth from this time and place, to friend and foe alike, that the torch has been passed to a new generation of Americans–born in this century, tempered by war, disciplined by a hard and bitter peace, proud of our ancient heritage–and unwilling to witness or permit the slow undoing of those human rights to which this nation has always been committed, and to which we are committed today at home and around the world.

Let every nation know, whether it wishes us well or ill, that we shall pay any price, bear any burden, meet any hardship, support any friend, oppose any foe to assure the survival and the success of liberty.

With the Soviet Union, as well as with Marxist philosophy, the United States faced two foes more dangerous than King George and Parliament. Referring to the American Revolution as an example of where Americans summoned the courage to resist a powerful enemy, President Kennedy found compelling inspiration. With these examples, he showed the world the superiority of "the first revolution" to the Bolshevik Revolution, which turned Russia into the Soviet Union. Kennedy believed our system of government and way of life were capable of spreading prosperity much more effectively than the Marxist system could ever hope to do.

★   ★   ★

Since this country was founded, each generation of Americans has been summoned to give testimony to its national loyalty. The graves of young Americans who answered the call to service surround the globe.

Now the trumpet summons us again—not as a call to bear arms, though arms we need—not as a call to battle, though embattled we are—but a call to bear the burden of a long twilight struggle, year in and year out, "rejoicing in hope, patient in tribulation"—a struggle against the common enemies of man: tyranny, poverty, disease and war itself.

Can we forge against these enemies a grand and global alliance, North and South, East and West, that can assure a more fruitful life for all mankind? Will you join in that historic effort?

President Kennedy's quotation is from the Bible: "Not slothful in business; fervent in spirit; serving the Lord; rejoicing in hope; patient in tribulation; continuing instant in prayer; distributing to the necessity of saints; given to hospitality" (Romans 12:12, KJV). Like many other great orators throughout history, President Kennedy drew upon the eloquence and resonance of a well-known literary reference to engage his audience.

In the long history of the world, only a few generations have been granted the role of defending freedom in its hour of maximum danger. I do not shrink from this responsibility—I welcome it. I do not believe that any of us would exchange places with any other people or any other generation. The energy, the faith, the devotion which we bring to this endeavor will light our country and all who serve it—and the glow from that fire can truly light the world.

And so, my fellow Americans: ask not what your country can do for you—ask what you can do for your country.

My fellow citizens of the world: ask not what America will do for you, but what together we can do for the freedom of man.

Finally, whether you are citizens of America or citizens of the world, ask of us here the same high standards of strength and sacrifice which we ask of you. With a good conscience our only sure reward, with history the final judge of our deeds, let us go forth to lead the land we love, asking His blessing and His help, but knowing that here on earth God's work must truly be our own.

Having cited the Declaration of Independence, President Kennedy called for a commitment from modern day Americans, which was similar to that made by our Founding Fathers—those who pledged their lives, their fortunes, and their sacred honor for the sake of freedom. During the 1950s and 1960s, the Soviet Union advanced communism—a political philosophy that was radically opposed to the values of the Declaration of Independence. As the Soviets attempted to spread their influence worldwide, President Kennedy—the then-new leader of the United States—spoke about preventing Soviet dominance, while winning the world to the American vision, which had been enshrined in our Declaration of Independence.

5

*Thus I consent, Sir, to this Constitution because
I expect no better, and because I am not sure,
that it is not the best.*

—BENJAMIN FRANKLIN

Benjamin Franklin, one of our most notable Founding Fathers, was the embodiment of a Renaissance man—an author, statesman, politician, philosopher, inventor, publisher and printer, scientist, soldier, and diplomat. Franklin espoused core American values: hard work, achievement, education, and thrift. He was one of the most successful, influential, and well-loved figures of his time, and his popularity has endured throughout the centuries.

He helped negotiate and write the 1783 Treaty of Paris which ended the Revolutionary War, and he was also a signer of the new Constitution in 1787. From May 25 to September 17, 1787, the Constitutional Convention was held in Philadelphia. Its purpose was to correct the Articles of Confederation, which was a loose set of laws that governed the United States at that time. Franklin attended the convention as a delegate from Pennsylvania, and on the last day, he wanted to give a speech. Too weak to deliver the speech himself, he had fellow Pennsylvanian James Wilson deliver it. By all standards, it is considered a masterpiece.

Benjamin Franklin's Speech before the Constitutional Convention, September 17, 1787

I confess that there are several parts of this constitution which I do not at present approve, but I am not sure I shall never approve them: For having lived long, I have experienced many instances of being obliged by better information, or fuller consideration, to change opinions even on important subjects, which I once thought right, but found to be otherwise. It is therefore that the older I grow, the more apt I am to doubt my own judgment, and to pay more respect to the judgment of others.

This may seem strange to begin talking *in favor* of the Constitution, but Franklin showed that his perspective was not utopian. He knew it was impossible to expect to create a perfect government, but he was correct that a good government was better than no government at all. Benjamin Franklin also offered a dose of the humility and wisdom for which he is esteemed. He stated that he had lived long enough to know that even the wisest people frequently change their opinions. Franklin said that he had learned to place substantial value on the judgment of those he trusted, indicating that he deferred to the wisdom of his colleagues.

In these sentiments, Sir, I agree to this Constitution with all its faults, if they are such; because I think a general Government necessary for us, and there is no form of Government but what may be a blessing to the people if well administered, and believe farther that this is likely to be well administered for a course of years, and can only end in Despotism, as other forms have done before it, when the people shall become so corrupted as to need despotic Government, being incapable of any other. I doubt too whether any other Convention we can obtain, may be able to make a better Constitution. For when you assemble a number of men to have the advantage of their joint wisdom, you inevitably assemble with those men, all their prejudices, their passions, their errors of opinion, their local interests, and their selfish views. From such an assembly can a perfect production be expected? It therefore astonishes me, Sir, to find this system approaching so near to perfection as it does; and I think it will astonish our enemies, who are waiting with confidence to hear that our councils are confounded like those of the Builders of Babel; and that our States are on the point of separation, only to meet hereafter for the purpose of cutting one another's throats. Thus I consent, Sir, to this Constitution because I expect no better, and because I am not sure, that it is not the best.

The reference to the "Builders of Babel" is found in Genesis 11. The Tower of Babel was designed to unite humanity and make a name for the city of Babel—a name greater than that of God. God did not approve of this kind of egotistical hubris, so He cursed the builders with different languages and scattered them abroad. This made it impossible for them to complete their project. Franklin pointed out that the attempt to formulate unity by the Continental Congress had succeeded, whether or not it was perfect, which meant they had beaten the odds.

★   ★   ★

Much of the strength & efficiency of any Government in procuring and securing happiness to the people, depends, on opinion, on the general opinion of the goodness of the Government, as well as of the wisdom and integrity of its Governors. I hope therefore that for our own sakes as a part of the people, and for the sake of posterity, we shall act heartily and unanimously in recommending this Constitution (if approved by Congress & confirmed by the Conventions) wherever our influence may extend, and turn our future thoughts & endeavors to the means of having it well administered.

Franklin was certain the federal government, established by the Constitution, would improve the lives of Americans and secure the future for subsequent generations. He recognized that with all of its flaws—whether real or imagined—each would be used to argue against ratifying the Constitution. It was clear that Ben Franklin was a consensus builder, which is why he pleaded with his fellow participants to provide a unified face in support of the document.

Franklin, thinking of future generations, recognized that even the most perfectly formed government on paper will go awry if it is not administered by people with integrity, honesty, and respect for the citizenry.

6

*I believe that it must be the policy of the
United States to support free peoples who are
resisting attempted subjugation by armed
minorities or by outside pressures.*
—HARRY TRUMAN

In the aftermath of World War II, the United States and the Soviet Union engaged in a nearly half-century-long political conflict called the Cold War. The Cold War was born from a disagreement between the former allies about how the world would be configured after World War II. The purpose of the Soviet Union was to spread communism throughout the world, and the United States established a containment policy to thwart its spread. Though the militaries of the United States and the USSR never officially clashed, the tense Cold War lasted for decades and only ended with the collapse of the Soviet Union in 1991.

The Truman Doctrine is the common name for the United States' strategy of containment. It was first presented by President Harry Truman in his address to Congress on March 12, 1947. Truman's address was precipitated by a visit to Washington DC in December 1946 by the Greek Prime Minister, Konstantinos

Tsaldaris, to ask for American financial aid. Should Greece fall, there would be little to prevent Turkey from yielding to the Soviet Union, and other nations falling after that. The United States agreed to send aid to Greece, and thus the United States officially embarked on its policy of the containment of communism.

The Truman Doctrine, March 12, 1947

The gravity of the situation which confronts the world today necessitates my appearance before a joint session of the Congress. The foreign policy and the national security of this country are involved.

Greece was in a dire economic situation, which compromised their national security, especially by being surrounded by communist countries. Great Britain had reached a point where it could no longer offer economic aid so it was necessary for the United States to fill the gap. Turkey was in similar danger, and the failure of either country would have been a victory for the expansion of communism and Soviet dominance. President Truman articulated a policy of containment for the Soviet Union and its allies.

One of the primary objectives of the foreign policy of the United States is the creation of conditions in which we and other nations will be able to work out a way of life free from coercion. This was a fundamental issue in the war with Germany and Japan. Our victory was won over countries which sought to impose their will, and their way of life, upon other nations.

In saying these words, President Truman stated that the threat to peace—which caused the United States to go to war in the first place—still existed. In the wake of the defeat of Germany and Japan, the Soviet Union had gained control and influence over many countries. Although this was not a declaration of war, it was a statement that warlike conditions actually existed between the two super-powers. Thus, "the cold war" became an appropriate name for this era.

At the present moment in world history nearly every nation must choose between alternative ways of life. The choice is too often not a free one.

One way of life is based upon the will of the majority, and is distinguished by free institutions, representative government, free elections, guarantees of individual liberty, freedom of speech and religion, and freedom from political oppression.

The second way of life is based upon the will of a minority forcibly imposed upon the majority. It relies upon terror and oppression, a controlled press and radio; fixed elections, and the suppression of personal freedoms.

I believe that it must be the policy of the United States to support free peoples who are resisting attempted subjugation by armed minorities or by outside pressures.

I believe that we must assist free peoples to work out their own destinies in their own way.

> I believe that our help should be primarily through economic
> and financial aid which is essential to economic stability
> and orderly political processes.

The preceding set the tone for how the United States would wage
"the cold war." While historians can argue over how well and how
fairly the Truman doctrine was implemented, the concept is consistent with principles dating back to the Declaration of Independence.
Being true to our heritage, the United States would help other nations to remain independent of Soviet dominance and oppression.

> It would be an unspeakable tragedy if these countries,
> which have struggled so long against overwhelming odds,
> should lose that victory for which they sacrificed so much.
> Collapse of free institutions and loss of independence
> would be disastrous not only for them but for the world.
> Discouragement and possibly failure would quickly be the
> lot of neighboring peoples striving to maintain their freedom
> and independence.

Truman's description of what would happen if the United States
failed to act was based on what the Soviets had done to East Germany and other Eastern European nations in the aftermath of
World War II. Rather than being free after years of struggle and
occupation, many countries that had suffered under Nazi occupation had become unwilling subjects to new masters—the Soviet
Union. President Truman did not want Greece, Turkey, or any
other country to meet the same fate. Furthermore, he recognized
that should the Soviet Union succeed in its expansionist policy,

the security of the United States would be threatened in the same way it was by Germany and Japan—two countries that the United States had sacrificed so much to defeat.

> The seeds of totalitarian regimes are nurtured by misery and want. They spread and grow in the evil soil of poverty and strife. They reach their full growth when the hope of a people for a better life has died. We must keep that hope alive.
>
> The free peoples of the world look to us for support in maintaining their freedoms.
>
> If we falter in our leadership, we may endanger the peace of the world—and we shall surely endanger the welfare of our own nation.
>
> Great responsibilities have been placed upon us by the swift movement of events.

President Truman realized that people in desperate circumstances are vulnerable to powerful politicians who offer to help but whose actions belie their true motives: to victimize these unfortunate people. He didn't want to see liberty and freedom destroyed across the world because nations were so desperate from poverty that they believed false promises made by rulers who would enslave them.

7

In 1787, the Constitutional Convention completed its work and the delegates went back to their home states to convince the American people to ratify this new Constitution. Almost immediately, this freshly crafted document was attacked by its opponents. Alexander Hamilton, John Jay and James Madison were prominent proponents for a strong national government. Between October 1787 and August 1788, these three men wrote a series of articles to persuade the people of New York to support ratification. These "papers," which were later published as a book known as *The Federalist Papers*, presented an explanation of the Constitution and the federal system, and specifically the ideals of justice, general welfare and the rights of individuals. To this day, *The Federalist Papers* are considered *the* primary source for understanding the U.S. Constitution.

Federalist No. 10 and Federalist No. 51 are the most famous of all.

James Madison wrote Federalist No. 10 to address how to guard against factions, known more commonly today as special interest groups.

Federalist No. 10, Part One, November 23, 1787

AMONG the numerous advantages promised by a well-constructed Union, none deserves to be more accurately developed than its tendency to break and control the violence of faction.

James Madison and other Founding Fathers worried that factions—special interest groups—would be the downfall of the newly formed United States of America. A faction that pursues its interests in a peaceful way is usually not a problem. The danger comes when a faction gains control of the government and uses the government to pursue its own interests at the expense of others. Protecting America against the dangers of factions was a preoccupation for many of the Founding Fathers.

The valuable improvements made by the American constitutions on the popular models, both ancient and modern, cannot certainly be too much admired; but it would be an unwarrantable partiality, to contend that they have as effectually obviated the danger on this side, as was wished and expected. Complaints are everywhere heard from our most considerate and virtuous citizens, equally the friends of public and private faith, and of public and personal liberty, that our governments are too unstable, that the public good is disregarded in the conflicts of rival parties, and that measures are too often decided, not according to the rules of justice and the rights of the minor party, but by the superior force of an interested and overbearing majority.

Many citizens feared that the Constitution gave too much power to the majority—power that could and would be abused and used to persecute the minority. These early Americans had lived through British oppression so they were naturally suspicious and thus were reluctant to form a new government, which would only empower another majority to oppress a minority.

It will be found, indeed, on a candid review of our situation, that some of the distresses under which we labor have been erroneously charged on the operation of our governments; but it will be found, at the same time, that other causes will not alone account for many of our heaviest misfortunes; and, particularly, for that prevailing and increasing distrust of public engagements, and alarm for private rights, which are echoed from one end of the continent to the other. These must be chiefly, if not wholly, effects of the unsteadiness and injustice with which a factious spirit has tainted our public administrations

Not only had Americans experienced corruption at the hands of the British government, but many had also experienced it with their state governments. James Madison suggested that the accounts of oppression by state governments, which made many Americans wary of the Constitution, had been blown out of proportion.

★   ★   ★

> By a faction, I understand a number of citizens, whether
> amounting to a majority or a minority of the whole, who are
> united and actuated by some common impulse of passion,
> or of interest, adversed to the rights of other citizens, or to
> the permanent and aggregate interests of the community.

Madison defined a faction as a group of people, large or small,
united by a common interest that violates the rights—any right—
of other citizens. In 21st century America, these would include
"special interest groups."

★   ★   ★

> The latent causes of faction are thus sown in the nature of
> man; and we see them everywhere brought into different
> degrees of activity, according to the different circumstances
> of civil society. A zeal for different opinions concerning
> religion, concerning government, and many other points,
> as well of speculation as of practice; an attachment to
> different leaders ambitiously contending for pre-eminence
> and power; or to persons of other descriptions whose
> fortunes have been interesting to the human passions, have,
> in turn, divided mankind into parties, inflamed them with
> mutual animosity, and rendered them much more disposed
> to vex and oppress each other than to co-operate for their
> common good.

Madison explained that factions are part of human nature. They
are caused by a person's tendency to have a preference for a cer-

tain religion, a certain type of government, or for certain leaders. He also explained that no government, regardless how effective, could change human nature. The only government worth having is a government that takes into account a person's unavoidable tendency to form factions and creates safeguards against it.

It is in vain to say that enlightened statesmen will be able to adjust these clashing interests, and render them all subservient to the public good. Enlightened statesmen will not always be at the helm. Nor, in many cases, can such an adjustment be made at all without taking into view indirect and remote considerations, which will rarely prevail over the immediate interest which one party may find in disregarding the rights of another or the good of the whole. The inference to which we are brought is, that the CAUSES of faction cannot be removed, and that relief is only to be sought in the means of controlling its EFFECTS.

James Madison was clear about the limits of what a government could do. It is simply impossible to pretend that a government can eliminate the causes of human evil. Likewise, it is useless to construct a government based on the theory that it will always be run by good people.

If a faction consists of less than a majority, relief is supplied by the republican principle, which enables the majority to defeat its sinister views by regular vote. It may clog the administration,

it may convulse the society; but it will be unable to execute and mask its violence under the forms of the Constitution. When a majority is included in a faction, the form of popular government, on the other hand, enables it to sacrifice to its ruling passion or interest both the public good and the rights of other citizens. To secure the public good and private rights against the danger of such a faction, and at the same time to preserve the spirit and the form of popular government, is then the great object to which our inquiries are directed.

Madison explained that minority factions aren't troublesome—that while they may cause temporary heartache, they would ultimately be defeated by the vote of the majority. Factions that are made up of a majority of people are truly concerning because these factions have the power to oppress. Madison said the government must be built so that it prevents a majority faction from abusing others under the mask of the Constitution.

8

A republic, by which I mean a government in which the scheme of representation takes place, opens a different prospect, and promises the cure for which we are seeking.
—JAMES MADISON

Federalist No. 10, Part Two, November 23, 1787

By what means is this object attainable? Evidently by one of two only. Either the existence of the same passion or interest in a majority at the same time must be prevented, or the majority, having such coexistent passion or interest, must be rendered, by their number and local situation, unable to concert and carry into effect schemes of oppression.

James Madison continued his discussion of factions by asking how a government could be created that would prevent a majority faction from abusing the minority. The first option—preventing a majority faction from ever forming—is not realistic. The second option is to make certain the government is structured in such a way that majority factions are prevented from using the government at the expense of others.

From this view of the subject it may be concluded that a pure democracy, by which I mean a society consisting of a small number of citizens, who assemble and administer the government in person, can admit of no cure for the mischiefs of faction. A common passion or interest will, in almost every case, be felt by a majority of the whole; a communication and concert result from the form of government itself; and there is nothing to check the inducements to sacrifice the weaker party or an obnoxious individual. Hence it is that such democracies have ever been spectacles of turbulence and contention; have ever been found incompatible with personal security or the rights of property; and have in general been as short in their lives as they have been violent in their deaths.

This is the problem of "the tyranny of the majority." Not only can the majority violate the rights of a minority, but such violations produce a backlash that destroy a democratic society. This means that, instead of having a peaceful government, purely democratic societies are marked by violence and instability.

A republic, by which I mean a government in which the scheme of representation takes place, opens a different prospect, and promises the cure for which we are seeking.

While the U.S. is commonly called a "democracy," the founders actually created a government that was intentionally *not* a democracy. They created a representative form of government called a *republic* because they believed this form of government offered solutions to all of the flaws of a democracy, including the "tyranny of the majority."

The two great points of difference between a democracy and a republic are: first, the delegation of the government, in the latter, to a small number of citizens elected by the rest; secondly, the greater number of citizens, and greater sphere of country, over which the latter may be extended.

There are two important differences between a republic and a democracy. First, in a republic, the people vote for representatives who vote on the laws. In a democracy, the people are the government and vote on the laws. Second, a democracy can only work in a very small country where it's possible to have *every* citizen vote on *every* issue. The larger the country grows, the more untenable a democracy becomes. A republic, by contrast, works better as the country grows larger.

The effect of the first difference is, on the one hand, to refine and enlarge the public views, by passing them through the medium of a chosen body of citizens, whose wisdom may best discern the true interest of their country, and whose patriotism and love of justice will be least likely to sacrifice it to temporary or partial considerations.

The Founders believed that a group of representatives, voted on by the people, would be a moral, wise, and patriotic filter through which the opinions of the people could be passed. Assuming this body of representatives is, in fact, moral, wise, and patriotic, it would be reasonable to assume that they would not pass laws based on a whim or for frivolous reasons.

In the first place, it is to be remarked that, however small the republic may be, the representatives must be raised to a certain number, in order to guard against the cabals of a few; and that, however large it may be, they must be limited to a certain number, in order to guard against the confusion of a multitude.

There was no exact way for the Founders to determine the right number of representatives, but the Founding Fathers generally knew that they needed a group large enough to keep each person accountable, but small enough to be workable, in the decision-making process.

In the next place, as each representative will be chosen by a greater number of citizens in the large than in the small republic, it will be more difficult for unworthy candidates to practice with success the vicious arts by which elections are too often carried; and the suffrages of the people being more free, will be more likely to centre in men who possess the most attractive merit and the most diffusive and established characters.

Another advantage of a large republic is that a greater number of citizens will prevent unworthy candidates from taking office. Madison based this argument on the principle that it's easy to fool a few people but much harder to fool a large group of people. The larger the body of voters, the more likely it would be that frauds would be exposed.

> The other point of difference is, the greater number of citizens and extent of territory which may be brought within the compass of republican than of democratic government; and it is this circumstance principally which renders factious combinations less to be dreaded in the former than in the latter.

Madison argued that because a large territory would create a large number of interests, it is unlikely that any one faction would be able to dominate the nation.

> Hence, it clearly appears that the same advantage which a republic has over a democracy, in controlling the effects of faction, is enjoyed by a large over a small republic,—is enjoyed by the Union over the States composing it.

Madison argued that just as a republic has many advantages over a democracy in controlling the negative effects of factions, so does a large Union have many advantages over the individual states in controlling the negative effects of a faction.

> In the extent and proper structure of the Union, therefore, we behold a republican remedy for the diseases most

incident to republican government. And according to the
degree of pleasure and pride we feel in being republicans,
ought to be our zeal in cherishing the spirit and supporting
the character of Federalists.

Madison concluded his case for the Constitution by restating his belief that a Union structured as a republic is the best type of government for preventing the evils of factions and special interest groups.
Since, at the time, all of the states were established republics—and
since Madison had demonstrated that the larger the republic, the
safer an individual's freedoms—he concluded that being part of a
greater republican structure, as established by the Constitution,
would offer individuals the ultimate protection from factions.

9

> *I have a dream that one day this nation*
> *will rise up and live out the true meaning*
> *of its creed: "We hold these truths to be self-evident:*
> *that all men are created equal.*
> —Martin Luther King, Jr.

Martin Luther King, Jr. was a Baptist minister and the most prominent civil rights advocate in U.S. history. For his work to peaceably end racial discrimination and segregation, Dr. King was awarded the Nobel Peace Prize in 1964. Though he was assassinated in 1968, his legacy today remains very much alive.

On August 28, 1963, King delivered what is considered one of the greatest speeches of all time from the steps of the Lincoln Memorial in Washington, DC. Over 200,000 people, who had participated in the March on Washington for "Jobs and Freedom," witnessed what many considered to be the most significant moment of the civil rights movement and one of the most profound speeches in American history.

"I Have a Dream"
by Martin Luther King, Jr., August 28, 1963

Five score years ago, a great American, in whose symbolic shadow we stand signed the Emancipation Proclamation. This momentous decree came as a great beacon light of hope to millions of Negro slaves who had been seared in the flames of withering injustice. It came as a joyous daybreak to end the long night of captivity.

But one hundred years later, we must face the tragic fact that the Negro is still not free. One hundred years later, the life of the Negro is still sadly crippled by the manacles of segregation and the chains of discrimination. One hundred years later, the Negro lives on a lonely island of poverty in the midst of a vast ocean of material prosperity. One hundred years later, the Negro is still languishing in the corners of American society and finds himself an exile in his own land. So we have come here today to dramatize an appalling condition.

The Emancipation Proclamation was an important part of how the Civil War came to liberate people who had never been granted equality before and who were still not given equal protection under the law a century later.

Now is the time to rise from the dark and desolate valley of segregation to the sunlit path of racial justice. Now is the time to open the doors of opportunity to all of God's children. Now is the time to lift our nation from the quicksands of racial injustice to the solid rock of brotherhood.

The emphasis of Dr. King's speech is on the word "now." Most of his listeners agreed with him that segregation needed to end because it was unjust. The problem he faced was not with those who disagreed with his principles, but with those who thought they should not yet practice those principles.

But there is something that I must say to my people who stand on the warm threshold which leads into the palace of justice. In the process of gaining our rightful place we must not be guilty of wrongful deeds. Let us not seek to satisfy our thirst for freedom by drinking from the cup of bitterness and hatred.

We must forever conduct our struggle on the high plane of dignity and discipline.

Like the Sons of Liberty before the outbreak of the Revolutionary War, the civil rights leadership faced the challenge of opposing unjust laws without allowing their opposition to cross the line into lawlessness. Dr. King saw the importance of avoiding retaliatory violence against persons and property, as well as clearly distancing his movement from any groups that might be prone to commit such acts.

I say to you today, my friends, that in spite of the difficulties and frustrations of the moment, I still have a dream. It is a dream deeply rooted in the American dream.

I have a dream that one day this nation will rise up and live out the true meaning of its creed: "We hold these truths to be self-evident: that all men are created equal."

> I have a dream that one day on the red hills of Georgia the sons of former slaves and the sons of former slaveowners will be able to sit down together at a table of brotherhood.

> I have a dream that one day even the state of Mississippi, a desert state, sweltering with the heat of injustice and oppression, will be transformed into an oasis of freedom and justice.

> I have a dream that my four children will one day live in a nation where they will not be judged by the color of their skin but by the content of their character.

In the most famous part of his speech, which has become well known worldwide, King invoked the power and heritage of the Declaration of Independence and the Bible. The New Testament explains several cases in which Jesus offended religious leaders because He was willing to sit and eat with the "wrong" people.

> I have a dream that one day every valley shall be exalted, every hill and mountain shall be made low, the rough places will be made plain, and the crooked places will be made straight, and the glory of the Lord shall be revealed, and all flesh shall see it together.

This quotation from the Old Testament Bible (Isaiah 40:4-5) prophesied the end of Babylonian captivity and the return of the Israelites to their land as a free people. His quotation may have been a hint that the powers that profited from segregation were going to be defeated and those who were powerless were going to be raised up to high positions.

This will be the day when all of God's children will be able
to sing with a new meaning, "My country, 'tis of thee, sweet
land of liberty, of thee I sing. Land where my fathers died,
land of the pilgrim's pride, from every mountainside, let
freedom ring."

Many American immigrants have taught their children to identify
with the Founding Fathers and even with the first Pilgrims who
colonized North America. King poignantly, and correctly, pointed
out that African-Americans had been excluded from the nation's
identity. In fact, they were made to feel less American than the
white descendants of more recent immigrants.

★   ★   ★

When we let freedom ring, when we let it ring from every
village and every hamlet, from every state and every city, we
will be able to speed up that day when all of God's children,
black men and white men, Jews and Gentiles, Protestants
and Catholics, will be able to join hands and sing in the
words of the old Negro spiritual, "Free at last! Free at last!
Thank God Almighty, we are free at last!"

African-Americans wanted to be able to sing, "My Country, 'Tis of
Thee." King invited all peoples of every background to sing along to
an old slave song. By ending segregation and other forms of societal
oppression, he suggested that everyone would be freed from bond-
age. As he rightly pointed out: "*All* people in a segregated society are
oppressed by that segregation, and all should long for freedom."

10

Federalist No. 51 was written by James Madison and, like Federalist No. 10, is considered to be one of the most famous of the *Federalist Papers* penned by our Founding Fathers. They were preoccupied with creating a system of checks and balances in the federal government, a system which would ensure the citizenry that no one person or group could grow powerful enough to control the entire government. In this Federalist paper, Madison made the original case for "checks and balances" and discussed how they should be created. Even though Federalist No. 51 was written over 200 years ago, it is still cited today by judges and lawmakers.

Federalist No. 51, February 6, 1788

TO WHAT expedient, then, shall we finally resort, for maintaining in practice the necessary partition of power among the several departments, as laid down in the Constitution? The only answer that can be given is, that as all these exterior provisions are found to be inadequate, the defect must be supplied, by so contriving the interior structure of the government as that its several constituent parts may, by their mutual relations, be the means of keeping each other in their proper places.

In this clause, it is pointed out that many of the Founders believed it was critically important for the federal government to have restraints in place that balanced the executive (presidency), legislative (Congress), and judicial (court system) branches.

In order to lay a due foundation for that separate and distinct exercise of the different powers of government, which to a certain extent is admitted on all hands to be essential to the preservation of liberty, it is evident that each department should have a will of its own; and consequently should be so constituted that the members of each should have as little agency as possible in the appointment of the members of the others.

According to the Founding Fathers, the function of the government depended on giving each branch as much autonomy as possible. That meant that members of each branch had as little input as possible concerning appointments to another branch of government.

It may be a reflection on human nature, that such devices should be necessary to control the abuses of government. But what is government itself, but the greatest of all reflections on human nature? If men were angels, no government would be necessary. If angels were to govern men, neither external nor internal controls on government would be necessary. In framing a government which is to be administered by men over men, the great difficulty lies in this: you must first enable the government to control the governed; and in the next place oblige it to control itself.

This is the paradoxical problem of government. Humans need government because humans are not "angels." However, humans are themselves the government. The poet Juvenal expressed it in the famous question: *Quis custodiet ipsos custodes?—Who watches the watchmen?*

There are, moreover, two considerations particularly applicable to the federal system of America, which place that system in a very interesting point of view.

First. In a single republic, all the power surrendered by the people is submitted to the administration of a single government; and the usurpations are guarded against by a division of the government into distinct and separate departments. In the compound republic of America, the power surrendered by the people is first divided between two distinct governments, and then the portion allotted to each subdivided among distinct and separate departments. Hence a double security arises to the rights of the people. The different governments will control each other, at the same time that each will be controlled by itself.

Second. It is of great importance in a republic not only to guard the society against the oppression of its rulers, but to guard one part of the society against the injustice of the other part. Different interests necessarily exist in different classes of citizens. If a majority be united by a common interest, the rights of the minority will be insecure. There are but two methods of providing against this evil: the one by creating a will in the community independent of the majority that is, of the society itself; the other, by comprehending in the society so many separate descriptions of citizens as will render an unjust combination of a majority of the whole very improbable, if not impracticable.

These two points basically make the claim that the government is most effective when divided up into many governments, thus the three branches of government, the division of the legislative branch into two houses, and the interplay between the state governments and the federal government.

Justice is the end of government. It is the end of civil society. It ever has been and ever will be pursued until it be obtained, or until liberty be lost in the pursuit. In a society under the forms of which the stronger faction can readily unite and oppress the weaker, anarchy may as truly be said to reign as in a state of nature, where the weaker individual is not secured against the violence of the stronger; and as, in the latter state, even the stronger individuals are prompted, by the uncertainty of their condition, to submit to a government which may protect the weak as well as themselves; so, in the former state, will the more powerful factions or parties be gradually induced, by a like motive, to wish for a government

which will protect all parties, the weaker as well as the more powerful.

One reason the Founders believed justice should be secured was because they believed justice was in everyone's best interests. An important feature of this paragraph is its acknowledgment that anarchy is not a society lacking government. On the contrary, anarchy can exist *because* of government—that it exists wherever anyone is free to exploit or violate anyone else. The government can thus cause anarchy as easily as it can stop it.

It is no less certain than it is important, notwithstanding the contrary opinions which have been entertained, that the larger the society, provided it lie within a practical sphere, the more duly capable it will be of self-government. And happily for the REPUBLICAN CAUSE, the practicable sphere may be carried to a very great extent, by a judicious modification and mixture of the FEDERAL PRINCIPLE.

The bigger the country or nation, the more easily a republic can be formed that will make it practically impossible for factions to gain control of the government. Such a republic will only work, however, if the separation of powers is preserved in the government.

11

> *What we demand . . . is that the world be made fit*
> *and safe to live in; and particularly that*
> *it be made safe for every peace-loving nation which,*
> *like our own, wishes to live its own life, determine*
> *its own institutions, be assured of justice and*
> *fair dealing by the other peoples of the world*
> *as against force and selfish aggression.*
> —WOODROW WILSON

By January 1918, the U.S. had been involved in World War I for nearly a year, and at this time, the end of the war was fast approaching. On January 8, President Wilson delivered a speech before a joint session of Congress in which he sought to reassure Americans that their sacrifices in World War I were for a just cause— for peace in Europe. Ten months later, when Germany surrendered, Wilson's Fourteen Points became the basis for the terms of surrender. What makes this speech unique is that it is the only speech by a nation fighting in World War I that explicitly states the goals and aims of that nation and the nation's reason for joining the war.

President Woodrow Wilson's
'Fourteen Points,' January 8, 1918

It will be our wish and purpose that the processes of peace, when they are begun, shall be absolutely open and that they shall involve and permit henceforth no secret understandings of any kind. The day of conquest and aggrandizement is gone by; so is also the day of secret covenants entered into in the interest of particular governments and likely at some unlooked-for moment to upset the peace of the world. It is this happy fact, now clear to the view of every public man whose thoughts do not still linger in an age that is dead and gone, which makes it possible for every nation whose purposes are consistent with justice and the peace of the world to avow nor or at any other time the objects it has in view.

We entered this war because violations of right had occurred which touched us to the quick and made the life of our own people impossible unless they were corrected and the world secure once for all against their recurrence. What we demand in this war, therefore, is nothing peculiar to ourselves. It is that the world be made fit and safe to live in; and particularly that it be made safe for every peace-loving nation which, like our own, wishes to live its own life, determine its own institutions, be assured of justice and fair dealing by the other peoples of the world as against force and selfish aggression. All the peoples of the world are in effect partners in this interest, and for our own part we see very clearly that unless justice be done to others it will not be done to us.

The most popular reason given for the U.S.'s involvement in World War I was the sinking of the British cruise ship, *The Lusitania*, off the coast of New York. Although that was the provocation, conventional thought argues that it happened in large part because of secret alliances which set up a situation where nations joined the war without having any idea what they were getting themselves into. Wilson expressed the sincere desire of the United States that all peoples of the world would be safe from the selfish aggressions of others. Some criticized Wilson's vision for being idealistic, but Wilson expressed a sentiment that has echoed throughout American history.

I. Open covenants of peace, openly arrived at, after which there shall be no private international understandings of any kind but diplomacy shall proceed always frankly and in the public view.

This first demand is directly related to the primary cause of World War I. President Wilson described in the introduction to his fourteen points that there must be no secret agreements permitted.

II. Absolute freedom of navigation upon the seas, outside territorial waters, alike in peace and in war, except as the seas may be closed in whole or in part by international action for the enforcement of international covenants.

The rule of law must protect all people equally. Restricting the freedom to sail is essentially an invasion and occupation of that portion of the ocean. This was a point of contention during World

War I, and Wilson attempted to settle the issue as the end of the war approached.

★   ★   ★

III. The removal, so far as possible, of all economic barriers and the establishment of an equality of trade conditions among all the nations consenting to the peace and associating themselves for its maintenance.

Here, President Wilson stated that peace among nations requires that the people from each nation be free to trade with one another.

★   ★   ★

IV. Adequate guarantees given and taken that national armaments will be reduced to the lowest point consistent with domestic safety.

When a nation begins to build weapons that would allow it to commit acts of aggression against its neighbors, it is a violation of peaceful relationships. Prior to World War II, Britain's Winston Churchill warned the world that Germany was rearming. His warning, however, fell on deaf ears, and because no one listened, Adolph Hitler was able to build a massive military force that wreaked havoc on the world, especially throughout Europe.

XIV. A general association of nations must be formed under specific covenants for the purpose of affording mutual guarantees of political independence and territorial integrity to great and small states alike.

In regard to these essential rectifications of wrong and assertions of right we feel ourselves to be intimate partners of all the governments and peoples associated together against the Imperialists. We cannot be separated in interest or divided in purpose. We stand together until the end.

Point XIV describes the establishment of the League of Nations, which was the forerunner of today's United Nations. The objective espoused by the writers was a court that could decide between nations as an alternative to going to war. President Wilson wanted to put an end to the practice of one nation invading another nation in order to gain territory. Operation Desert Storm is a contemporary example in which this principle was put into practice: Iraq invaded Kuwait, and the nations responded by combining and restoring Kuwait as a nation.

12

The U.S. Constitution is the supreme law of the land. Adopted on September 17, 1787, the Constitution establishes the authority for the federal government and contains the framework for the structure of the government. It is the most sacred, authoritative, and respected document in America, and describes how the federal government is to act in concert with state governments and the citizenry.

The United States Constitution, Part One, September 17, 1787

We the People of the United States, in Order to form a more perfect Union, establish Justice, insure domestic Tranquility, provide for the common defence, promote the general Welfare, and secure the Blessings of Liberty to ourselves and our Posterity, do ordain and establish this Constitution for the United States of America.

The preamble of the Constitution is one of the most recognizable sentences in American history. Although it is not part of the legal document, in this one sentence the Founders described the purpose of the government and the vision for the country.

Article I. Legislative Branch
Section 1.

All legislative Powers herein granted shall be vested in a Congress of the United States, which shall consist of a Senate and House of Representatives.

This first section establishes the Senate and the House of Representatives as the sole authorities to legislate law. It does not give the executive branch—i.e., the president—the power to make laws. Presidents since that time, especially the more recent ones, have moved into this area with executive orders that are essentially the same as new laws, or the effect of a bill that has been passed by Congress and which he is signing into law.

★   ★   ★

Section 8.

Clause 1: The Congress shall have Power To lay and collect Taxes, Duties, Imposts and Excises, to pay the Debts and provide for the common Defence and general Welfare of the United States; but all Duties, Imposts and Excises shall be uniform throughout the United States;

In Section 8, it is clear that the Founders did not want one part of the United States to be treated unequally from any other part. Otherwise, one part of the country could impose special taxes on another part of the country. This section was later supplemented by the 16th Amendment, which permitted Congress to levy an income tax.

Clause 2: To borrow Money on the credit of the United States;

The Framers gave Congress the exclusive authority to put the United States in debt. However, they did not foresee the creation of a quasi-private agency like the Federal Reserve—established some 130 years later in 1913—taking over this responsibility.

Clause 3: To regulate Commerce with foreign Nations, and among the several States, and with the Indian Tribes;

Regulating commerce with foreign nations has increasingly become the province of the executive branch because it involves negotiating foreign treaties. But this is not what was envisioned by the Constitution.

Clause 4: To establish a uniform Rule of Naturalization, and uniform Laws on the subject of Bankruptcies throughout the United States;

Here, in Clause 4, the Founders are stating that it is the Congress, not any agency or department within the federal government, who is given the authority to make uniform laws about bankruptcies.

Clause 5: To coin Money, regulate the Value thereof, and of foreign Coin, and fix the Standard of Weights and Measures;

Clause 6: To provide for the Punishment of counterfeiting the Securities and current Coin of the United States;

These clauses have been used to justify the government's issuing and using paper money that is not backed by any commodity. This clearly was not the original intent.

Clause 8: To promote the Progress of Science and useful Arts, by securing for limited Times to Authors and Inventors the exclusive Right to their respective Writings and Discoveries;

The way the Constitution envisioned the government promoting science and art is by giving Congress the power to grant to authors and inventors exclusive rights to their writings, inventions, and intellectual properties.

Clause 9: To constitute Tribunals inferior to the supreme Court;

The president is not authorized to set up courts. Only Congress can establish them.

Clause 10: To define and punish Piracies and Felonies committed on the high Seas, and Offences against the Law of Nations;

Clause 11: To declare War, grant Letters of Marque and Reprisal, and make Rules concerning Captures on Land and Water;

Clauses 10 and 11 vest the legislative branch with all authority not only to declare war, but also to set penalties for foreign or international crimes. Congress is also the authority that sets policy about prisoners of war or disarmed enemy forces.

Clause 12: To raise and support Armies, but no Appropriation of Money to that Use shall be for a longer Term than two Years;

Even with the separation of powers, the Founders were worried about what any one branch of the government could or might do if the military were in its control. Here, the Constitution clearly authorizes Congress to fund the military, but it limits that funding to two years.

Clause 13: To provide and maintain a Navy;

Clause 14: To make Rules for the Government and Regulation of the land and naval Forces;

Clause 15: To provide for calling forth the Militia to execute the Laws of the Union, suppress Insurrections and repel Invasions;

Clause 16: To provide for organizing, arming, and disciplining, the Militia, and for governing such Part of them as may be employed in the Service of the United States, reserving to the States respectively, the Appointment of the Officers, and the Authority of training the Militia according to the discipline prescribed by Congress;

While the president is commander-in-chief of the military, Clauses 13-16 make clear that Congress still has the power to regulate the military. The modern idea that the president is primarily in control of the military, and that Congress' only role is to comply with the president's requests for funding, is contrary to the Founders' intent.

Clause 17: To exercise exclusive Legislation in all Cases whatsoever, over such District (not exceeding ten Miles square) as may, by Cession of particular States, and the Acceptance of Congress, become the Seat of the Government of the United States, and to exercise like Authority over all Places purchased by the Consent of the Legislature of the State in which the Same shall be, for the Erection of Forts, Magazines, Arsenals, dock-Yards, and other needful Buildings

This clause gives Congress authority over limited geographical areas that are "needed" by the federal government. It does not envision nor suggest huge areas of federal land whereby the government would become the ex-officio "plantation master."

★   ★   ★

Clause 18: To make all Laws which shall be necessary and proper for carrying into Execution the foregoing Powers, and all other Powers vested by this Constitution in the Government of the United States, or in any Department or Officer thereof.

Clause 18 grants Congress the sole authority to make all laws and to make what laws are necessary to carry out any of their powers.

13

This Constitution, and the Laws of the United States which shall be made in Pursuance thereof; and all Treaties made, or which shall be made, under the Authority of the United States, shall be the supreme Law of the Land; and the Judges in every State shall be bound thereby, any Thing in the Constitution or Laws of any State to the Contrary notwithstanding.
—THE U.S. CONSTITUTION

The United States Constitution, Part Two
Article II. Executive Branch
Section 1

Clause 1: The executive Power shall be vested in a President of the United States of America. He shall hold his Office during the Term of four Years

The president is elected to execute the powers of the government, but according to the Constitution, the president's power is limited.

He does not legislate. Only a four-year term is allowed before a new election is mandated. Until 1951, before the ratification of the 22nd Amendment, there was no limit to how many terms a person could serve as president. The only president serving more than two terms was Franklin Roosevelt, who served four.

Section 2.

Clause 1: The President shall be Commander in Chief of the Army and Navy of the United States, and of the Militia of the several States, when called into the actual Service of the United States; he may require the Opinion, in writing, of the principal Officer in each of the executive Departments, upon any Subject relating to the Duties of their respective Offices, and he shall have Power to grant Reprieves and Pardons for Offences against the United States, except in Cases of Impeachment.

The president is the commander of the military. The Founders knew that it was impossible to run an army by committee. The Constitution does not take for granted that being "Commander in Chief" means the president has automatic powers. The Constitution actually spells out that the president "may require the Opinion, in writing" rather than assuming such power is included in the office.

Clause 2: He shall have Power, by and with the Advice and Consent of the Senate, to make Treaties, provided two thirds of the Senators present concur; and he shall nominate, and by and with the Advice and Consent of the Senate, shall

appoint Ambassadors, other public Ministers and Consuls, Judges of the Supreme Court, and all other Officers of the United States, whose Appointments are not herein otherwise provided for, and which shall be established by Law: but the Congress may by Law vest the Appointment of such inferior Officers, as they think proper, in the President alone, in the Courts of Law, or in the Heads of Departments.

The Senate originally consisted of members appointed by the state governments. Now they are chosen in general state elections. They hold a special role in providing a check on the power of the president when it comes to making treaties.

Clause 3: The President shall have Power to fill up all Vacancies that may happen during the Recess of the Senate, by granting Commissions which shall expire at the End of their next Session.

The president does not have the power to fill vacancies in the democratically elected House of Representatives, only in the Senate.

Article III. Judicial Branch
Section 1.

The judicial Power of the United States shall be vested in one supreme Court, and in such inferior Courts as the Congress may from time to time ordain and establish. The Judges, both of the supreme and inferior Courts, shall hold their Offices during good Behaviour, and shall, at stated

Times, receive for their Services, a Compensation, which shall not be diminished during their Continuance in Office.

The independence of the judicial branch is protected by making the office of judge a lifetime appointment and by stating that the pay for judges may not be reduced while they are in office.

Section 2.

Clause 1: The judicial Power shall extend to all Cases, in Law and Equity, arising under this Constitution, the Laws of the United States, and Treaties made, or which shall be made, under their Authority;–to all Cases affecting Ambassadors, other public Ministers and Consuls;–to all Cases of admiralty and maritime Jurisdiction;–to Controversies to which the United States shall be a Party;–to Controversies between two or more States;–between a State and Citizens of another State;–between Citizens of different States, – between Citizens of the same State claiming Lands under Grants of different States, and between a State, or the Citizens thereof, and foreign States, Citizens or Subjects.

This clause grants the judicial branch oversight for all possible controversies. The Eleventh Amendment was enacted to reduce the scope of this clause so that it did not include "any suit in law or equity, commenced or prosecuted against one of the United States by Citizens of another State, or by Citizens or Subjects of any Foreign State."

Section 3.

Clause 1: Treason against the United States shall consist only in levying War against them, or in adhering to their Enemies,

giving them Aid and Comfort. No Person shall be convicted
of Treason unless on the Testimony of two Witnesses to the
same overt Act, or on Confession in open Court.

The Founders were worried that the government would misuse
its power to punish any disagreement by calling it "treason." So,
they carefully limited what was considered treason and what was
necessary to convict a person of treason. The demand for "the Testimony of two Witnesses" comes from the Bible (see Deuteronomy
17:6; Matthew 18:16).

Article IV
Section 1.

Full Faith and Credit shall be given in each State to the
public Acts, Records, and judicial Proceedings of every other
State. And the Congress may by general Laws prescribe the
Manner in which such Acts, Records and Proceedings shall
be proved, and the Effect thereof.

This clause is pretty straightforward: that each state is to accept
the records from other states, including marriage licenses.

Section 4.

Clause 2: This Constitution, and the Laws of the United
States which shall be made in Pursuance thereof; and all
Treaties made, or which shall be made, under the Authority
of the United States, shall be the supreme Law of the Land;
and the Judges in every State shall be bound thereby,
any Thing in the Constitution or Laws of any State to the
Contrary notwithstanding.

Treaties made with other countries are extremely important because they are "the supreme Law of the Land." They bind everyone to abide by the stipulations in the treaty rather than to any
provisions in the laws of Congress or even the Constitution.

Clause 3: The Senators and Representatives before
mentioned, and the Members of the several State
Legislatures, and all executive and judicial Officers, both of
the United States and of the several States, shall be bound
by Oath or Affirmation, to support this Constitution; but no
religious Test shall ever be required as a Qualification to any
Office or public Trust under the United States.

This clause, not the First Amendment, guarantees that the federal
government is a secular institution. There is no requirement that
one be of any religious faith in order to hold office in the federal
government.

14

> *It is rather for us the living . . . that we here highly resolve that these dead shall not have died in vain, that this nation shall have a new birth of freedom, and that government of the people, by the people, for the people shall not perish from the earth.*
> —Abraham Lincoln

The Gettysburg Address, November 19, 1863

In July 1863, the Battle of Gettysburg was fought in and around Gettysburg, Pennsylvania. Considered the turning point of the Civil War, it stopped General Robert E. Lee's Army of Northern Virginia from invading the North. Four months later, on November 19, 1863, President Lincoln delivered a brief but profound address at the dedication of the Soldiers' National Cemetery at Gettysburg. Though the speech lasted just over two minutes, it is one of the most powerful and inspiring in American history as it reiterates the founding principles of America.

Now we are engaged in a great civil war, testing whether that nation, or any nation so conceived and so dedicated, can long endure. We are met on a great battlefield of that war. We have come to dedicate a portion of it, as a final resting place for those who died here, that the nation might live. This we may, in all propriety do. But in a larger sense, we cannot dedicate, we cannot consecrate, we cannot hallow, this ground. The brave men, living and dead, who struggled here, have hallowed it, far above our poor power to add or detract. The world will little note, nor long remember what we say here; while it can never forget what they did here.

It is rather for us the living, we here be dedicated to the great task remaining before us—that from these honored dead we take increased devotion to that cause for which they here gave the last full measure of devotion—that we here highly resolve that these dead shall not have died in vain, that this nation shall have a new birth of freedom, and that government of the people, by the people, for the people shall not perish from the earth.

In this short, but amazingly effective speech, President Lincoln took the idea of the dedication of the land at Gettysburg and turned it around. Rather than the people gathering to dedicate the land, Lincoln pronounced the land already dedicated by the sacrifice of those who fought and died. He said this battlefield could now be used to dedicate the people to continue the struggle for the principles of the nation—freedom and liberty, "…that government of the people, by the people, for the people…" restates the importance of *all* people being represented—an expansion of the Declaration of Independence.

The Emancipation Proclamation

The Emancipation Proclamation is composed of two proclamations issued by President Lincoln. The first, issued September 22, 1862, declared as free, all slaves of any of the Confederate States of America that did not return to Union authority by the start of 1863. The second, issued January 1, 1863, listed the ten specific states where slaves would be free. Though the proclamation did not expressly make slavery illegal, or even free slaves in the entire country, it laid the groundwork for the Thirteenth Amendment, which, when passed in 1865, made slavery illegal.

"That on the 1st day of January, A.D. 1863, all persons held as slaves within any State or designated part of a State the people whereof shall then be in rebellion against the United States shall be then, thenceforward, and forever free; and the executive government of the United States, including the military and naval authority thereof, will recognize and maintain the freedom of such persons and will do no act or acts to repress such persons, or any of them, in any efforts they may make for their actual freedom.

This part of the proclamation left those slaves living in states that had sided with the Union still in slavery. Oddly enough, it only granted freedom to slaves in the states that had seceded from the Union. Nevertheless, this was a significant turning point, marking the beginning of the process through which the Civil War abolished slavery. It also made it clear that escaped slaves from the Confederate states were to be treated as free men and women.

"That the executive will on the 1st day of January aforesaid, by proclamation, designate the States and parts of States, if any, in which the people thereof, respectively, shall then be in rebellion against the United States; and the fact that any State or the people thereof shall on that day be in good faith represented in the Congress of the United States by members chosen thereto at elections wherein a majority of the qualified voters of such States shall have participated shall, in the absence of strong countervailing testimony, be deemed conclusive evidence that such State and the people thereof are not then in rebellion against the United States."

This section set up the authority and procedure for deciding which states were in rebellion against the United States and which were not. Lincoln gave himself the authority to make that determination, but he also spelled out his primary means of making his decision.

And I hereby enjoin upon the people so declared to be free to abstain from all violence, unless in necessary self-defence; and I recommend to them that, in all case when allowed, they labor faithfully for reasonable wages.

Lincoln knew that critics, whether in the North or South, would accuse him of encouraging violence on the part of blacks against whites. He made sure to mention that both violence and theft were to be considered unacceptable on the part of the slaves who wanted to be free.

And I further declare and make known that such persons of suitable condition will be received into the armed service of the United States to garrison forts, positions, stations, and other places, and to man vessels of all sorts in said service.

While many slaves in Confederate states could not take advantage of the freedom declared in the Emancipation Proclamation, those living near a federal fort or near the border were able to take advantage of the President's declaration and find aid in their escape to a free state.

15

The powers not delegated to the United States by the Constitution, nor prohibited by it to the States, are reserved to the States respectively, or to the people.
—ARTICLE X, THE BILL OF RIGHTS

The first ten amendments to the Constitution are called the Bill of Rights. James Madison presented them to the first Congress in 1789 as an article. And although Madison is considered the chief architect and author, it is worth noting that George Mason was the driving force behind the document, having written the first draft. Mason was also the author of the 1776 Virginia Declaration of Rights, which The Bill of Rights was patterned after. As a leader of the Anti-Federalists, his objections led to the first 10 amendments. These ten amendments were ratified by three-fourths of the states in 1791 and became law. Because of ideological divisions between those for and those against the Constitution—among them, Mason—the Founders recognized that the Constitution was in jeopardy of not being ratified. Madison wrote the Bill of Rights to appeal to the Constitution's opponents, who believed the Constitution would take away individual freedoms and liberties. Today, The Bill of Rights is as central to American law and government as the Constitution itself.

The Bill of Rights
ARTICLES IN ADDITION TO, AND AMENDMENTS
OF, THE CONSTITUTION OF THE UNITED STATES
OF AMERICA, PROPOSED BY CONGRESS, AND
RATIFIED BY THE LEGISLATURES OF THE
SEVERAL STATES, PURSUANT TO THE FIFTH
ARTICLE OF THE ORIGINAL CONSTITUTION

★　　★　　★

Article [I.]
Congress shall make no law respecting an establishment of religion, or prohibiting the free exercise thereof; or abridging the freedom of speech, or of the press; or the right of the people peaceably to assemble, and to petition the Government for a redress of grievances.

At this time, some of the states still had official state-sanctioned churches. This clause was added because some feared the federal government might establish a national mandatory church because of the abuses in England. It was not because they felt that the government should ever totally separate itself from God or religion. In fact, the clause specifically allows for the free exercise of religion as well as freedom of speech, assembly and redress. Certainly, the application of this amendment has widened since it was first written. Originally, this amendment restricted only the federal government and not state law.

Article [II.]

A well regulated Militia, being necessary to the security of a free State, the right of the people to keep and bear Arms, shall not be infringed.

This amendment gives citizens the right to possess firearms whether they are part of a militia or for their own protection. Thomas Jefferson was a strong supporter of the Second Amendment, stating: "The beauty of the **second amendment** is that it will not be needed until they try to take it."

Article [III.]

No Soldier shall, in time of peace be quartered in any house, without the consent of the Owner, nor in time of war, but in a manner to be prescribed by law.

This article stipulates clearly that citizens are guaranteed that the military cannot treat the property of others as if it is their own, whether in peace or war-time. If civilian houses are needed, soldiers must follow legal procedures. They may not simply stay in someone's house just because they are part of the military.

Article [IV.]

The right of the people to be secure in their persons, houses, papers, and effects, against unreasonable searches and seizures, shall not be violated, and no Warrants shall issue, but upon probable cause, supported by Oath or affirmation, and particularly describing the place to be searched, and the persons or things to be seized.

Government agents are not permitted to search a home for evidence based on their own authority. They must have a documented reason—a warrant—stating what they are looking for and showing probable cause to believe that criminal activity is occurring at the place to be searched or that evidence of a crime may be found there.

Article [V.]

No person shall be held to answer for a capital, or otherwise infamous crime, unless on a presentment or indictment of a Grand Jury, except in cases arising in the land or naval forces, or in the Militia, when in actual service in time of War or public danger; nor shall any person be subject for the same offence to be twice put in jeopardy of life or limb; nor shall be compelled in any criminal case to be a witness against himself, nor be deprived of life, liberty, or property, without due process of law; nor shall private property be taken for public use, without just compensation.

Except in times of great emergency, there is a procedure the government must follow to make certain it is not acting in an arbitrary way. Also, the government has only one opportunity to convict a person of a crime, insuring that government officials and courts cannot bring a person to trial repeatedly until they obtain the verdict they desire.

Article [VI.]

In all criminal prosecutions, the accused shall enjoy the right to a speedy and public trial, by an impartial jury of the State and district wherein the crime shall have been committed, which district shall have been previously ascertained by law, and to be informed of the nature and cause of the accusation; to be confronted with the witnesses against him; to have compulsory process for obtaining witnesses in his favor, and to have the Assistance of Counsel for his defence.

This Article takes away from the government the ability to use secret trials. It also sets up safeguards to allow the accused to defend him or her self.

Article [VII.]

In Suits at common law, where the value in controversy shall exceed twenty dollars, the right of trial by jury shall be preserved, and no fact tried by a jury, shall be otherwise re-examined in any Court of the United States, than according to the rules of the common law.

While the Sixth Amendment acknowledges the right to a jury for criminal cases, the same right is guaranteed for lawsuits.

Article [VIII.]

Excessive bail shall not be required, nor excessive fines imposed, nor cruel and unusual punishments inflicted.

This is the simplest amendment to understand, though what counts as "excessive," "cruel," or "unusual" is open for debate.

Article [IX.]

The enumeration in the Constitution, of certain rights, shall not be construed to deny or disparage others retained by the people.

The Bill of Rights acknowledges some of the rights a person has, but it does not mention all of them. However, just because a right is not mentioned is not evidence that it can be denied.

Article [X.]

The powers not delegated to the United States by the Constitution, nor prohibited by it to the States, are reserved to the States respectively, or to the people.

The Constitution grants specific powers to the federal government of the United States. The federal government has since acquired some powers reserved to the States, such as education, welfare, retirement, etc. The Tenth Amendment does not specify which powers are *delegated* to the federal government or which ones are *prohibited* to the states. And it doesn't state which ones are *reserved* to the states or to the people. However, it is clear from the first sentence of Article 1, Section 1, of the Constitution ("All legislative Powers herein granted....") these rights, or powers, are defined in the doctrine of enumerated powers, which is the central focus of the Constitution. What our Constitution tells us is that power resides first and foremost in the people. The people then have the right to *delegate* their power, *reserve* it, or *prohibit* its exercise—not immediately through elections, but institutionally through the Constitution. The "power of the people" cannot be overstated, for it is the foundation of whatever legitimacy our system of government can claim. What the Tenth Amendment says, in summary, is this: *If a power has not been delegated to the federal government, that government simply does not have it.*

16

> *There is not a man beneath the canopy of heaven that does not know that slavery is wrong for him.*
> —FREDERICK DOUGLASS

Frederick Douglass, a former slave turned abolitionist, is one of the most prominent figures in United States history. As an author, minister, orator, and statesman, Douglass spent much of his time traveling the United States to speak about equality for all people, regardless of race, nationality, or gender. On July 5, 1852, Douglass gave one of the most famous and moving speeches in American history at an event in Rochester, New York, commemorating the signing of the Declaration of Independence.

'The Meaning of July Fourth for the Negro,' by Frederick Douglass, July 5, 1852

Fellow Citizens, I am not wanting in respect for the fathers of this republic. The signers of the Declaration of Independence were brave men. They were great men, too great enough to give frame to a great age. It does not often

> happen to a nation to raise, at one time, such a number of truly great men. The point from which I am compelled to view them is not, certainly, the most favorable; and yet I cannot contemplate their great deeds with less than admiration. They were statesmen, patriots and heroes, and for the good they did, and the principles they contended for, I will unite with you to honor their memory....

Douglass had good reason to be angry at the double standard assumed by the Founding Fathers, but he chose to build on their strengths rather than condemn them for their weaknesses. He argued that the problem with the Founders was not with their principles but that those principles needed to be applied to all people. Douglass stressed that everyone should have confidence in the principles for which the Founding Fathers fought and died.

> Fellow-citizens, above your national, tumultuous joy, I hear the mournful wail of millions whose chains, heavy and grievous yesterday, are, to-day, rendered more intolerable by the jubilee shouts that reach them. If I do forget, if I do not faithfully remember those bleeding children of sorrow this day, "may my right hand forget her cunning, and may my tongue cleave to the roof of my mouth!" To forget them, to pass lightly over their wrongs, and to chime in with the popular theme, would be treason most scandalous and shocking, and would make me a reproach before God and the world. My subject, then, fellow-citizens, is American slavery. I shall see this day and its popular characteristics from the slave's point of view. Standing

there identified with the American bondman, making his wrongs mine, I do not hesitate to declare, with all my soul, that the character and conduct of this nation never looked blacker to me than on this 4th of July!

Douglass quoted from Psalm 137 in the Old Testament Bible, which describes the Israelites' reaction to being taken captive to Babylon. It reads in part:

> "By the rivers of Babylon, there we sat down, yea, we wept, when we remembered Zion. We hanged our harps upon the willows in the midst thereof. For there they that carried us away captive required of us a song; and they that wasted us required of us mirth, saying, 'Sing us one of the songs of Zion.' How shall we sing the LORD's song in a strange land? If I forget thee, O Jerusalem, let my right hand forget her cunning. If I do not remember thee, let my tongue cleave to the roof of my mouth; if I prefer not Jerusalem above my chief joy" (KJV).

In doing so, Douglass drew on a common Christian heritage shared by both blacks and whites.

Would you have me argue that man is entitled to liberty? that he is the rightful owner of his own body? You have already declared it. Must I argue the wrongfulness of slavery? Is that a question for Republicans? Is it to be settled by the rules of logic and argumentation, as a matter beset with great difficulty, involving a doubtful application of the principle

of justice, hard to be understood? How should I look to-day, in the presence of Amercans, dividing, and subdividing a discourse, to show that men have a natural right to freedom? speaking of it relatively and positively, negatively and affirmatively. To do so, would be to make myself ridiculous, and to offer an insult to your understanding. There is not a man beneath the canopy of heaven that does not know that slavery is wrong for him.

Douglass appealed to the principles Americans all hold dear: freedom, liberty, and justice. He reasoned that people with such a heritage should not need to be convinced that slavery is wrong.

What, to the American slave, is your 4th of July? I answer; a day that reveals to him, more than all other days in the year, the gross injustice and cruelty to which he is the constant victim. To him, your celebration is a sham; your boasted liberty, an unholy license; your national greatness, swelling vanity; your sounds of rejoicing are empty and heartless; your denunciation of tyrants, brass fronted impudence; your shouts of liberty and equality, hollow mockery; your prayers and hymns, your sermons and thanksgivings, with all your religious parade and solemnity, are, to Him, mere bombast, fraud, deception, impiety, and hypocrisy—a thin veil to cover up crimes which would disgrace a nation of savages. There is not a nation on the earth guilty of practices more shocking and bloody than are the people of the United States, at this very hour.

The problem with standing up for great principles is that the crime of hypocrisy becomes all the greater when one refuses to practice those principles. By championing "the right to life, liberty, and the pursuit of happiness," Douglass argued that Americans were making the crime of slavery more obvious and perverse.

Allow me to say, in conclusion, notwithstanding the dark picture I have this day presented, of the state of the nation, I do not despair of this country. There are forces in operation which must inevitably work the downfall of slavery. "The arm of the Lord is not shortened," and the doom of slavery is certain. I, therefore, leave off where I began, with hope. While drawing encouragement from "the Declaration of Independence," the great principles it contains, and the genius of American Institutions, my spirit is also cheered by the obvious tendencies of the age.

Although not an exact Bible quotation, Mr. Douglass invokes language from Numbers 11:23 from the Old Testament. God promises to feed the people of Israel, and Moses finds the promise hard to believe. In verse 22, he asks, "Would they have enough if flocks and herds were slaughtered for them? Would they have enough if all the fish in the sea were caught for them?" Then, in verse 23, the passage reads: "The LORD answered Moses, 'Is the LORD's arm too short? You will now see whether or not what I say will come true for you.'"

Despite the critical and depressing rhetoric of the speech, Douglass ended on a note of hope. He looked forward to a future in which slavery would be abolished and all people would enjoy freedom and equality.

17

> *It is, indeed, little else than a name, where the government is too feeble to withstand the enterprises of faction, to confine each member of the society within the limits prescribed by the laws, and to maintain all in the secure and tranquil enjoyment of the rights of person and property.*
> —GEORGE WASHINGTON

President Washington's Farewell Address was first published on September 19, 1796. It reflects some of his most profound thoughts about America, the Constitution, American politics, and America's future after his service to the country—which spanned nearly a half-century. Washington originally prepared the letter, with the help of James Madison, in 1792, at the close of his first term in office. He put the letter aside when he decided to run for a second term. He revisited the letter four years later, and, with the help of Alexander Hamilton, created what is still considered to be one of the most thoughtful, well-expressed statements about America.

President George Washington's Farewell Address, Part One, September 17, 1796

The unity of Government, which constitutes you one people, is also now dear to you. It is justly so; for it is a main pillar in the edifice of your real independence, the support of your tranquillity at home, your peace abroad; of your safety; of your prosperity; of that very Liberty, which you so highly prize. But as it is easy to foresee, that, from different causes and from different quarters, much pains will be taken, many artifices employed, to weaken in your minds the conviction of this truth; as this is the point in your political fortress against which the batteries of internal and external enemies will be most constantly and actively (though often covertly and insidiously) directed, it is of infinite moment, that you should properly estimate the immense value of your national Union to your collective and individual happiness; that you should cherish a cordial, habitual, and immovable attachment to it; accustoming yourselves to think and speak of it as of the Palladium of your political safety and prosperity; watching for its preservation with jealous anxiety; discountenancing whatever may suggest even a suspicion, that it can in any event be abandoned; and indignantly frowning upon the first dawning of every attempt to alienate any portion of our country from the rest, or to enfeeble the sacred ties which now link together the various parts.

Washington spoke from personal experience, having risked his life to fight for independence from Britain. Victory depended on the colonies pulling together and fighting as one nation. He anticipated that without a unifying government, the states would grow apart and eventually even wage war against one another. He also foresaw that such weakness would make individual states easy prey for European empires.

In contemplating the causes, which may disturb our Union, it occurs as matter of serious concern, that any ground should have been furnished for characterizing parties by Geographical discriminations, Northern and Southern, Atlantic and Western; whence designing men may endeavour to excite a belief, that there is a real difference of local interests and views. One of the expedients of party to acquire influence, within particular districts, is to misrepresent the opinions and aims of other districts. You cannot shield yourselves too much against the jealousies and heart-burnings, which spring from these misrepresentations; they tend to render alien to each other those, who ought to be bound together by fraternal affection.

Obviously, this warning turned out to be prophetic, since regional loyalties did eventually cause a war and attempted to end the Union. To combat this tendency, Washington asked his listeners to resist resentment, and instead, bind themselves to the other parts of the country in brotherly love.

To the efficacy and permanency of your Union, a Government for the whole is indispensable. No alliances, however strict, between the parts can be an adequate substitute; they must inevitably experience the infractions and interruptions, which all alliances in all times have experienced. Sensible of this momentous truth, you have improved upon your first essay, by the adoption of a Constitution of Government better calculated than your former for an intimate Union, and for the efficacious management of your common concerns. This Government, the offspring of our own choice, uninfluenced and unawed, adopted upon full investigation and mature deliberation, completely free in its principles, in the distribution of its powers, uniting security with energy, and containing within itself a provision for its own amendment, has a just claim to your confidence and your support. Respect for its authority, compliance with its laws, acquiescence in its measures, are duties enjoined by the fundamental maxims of true Liberty.

As the first president under the Constitution, Washington came to the office with fame and respect from every region of the country. He was a true national celebrity. For this reason, when he left office, it was a real test for the young nation. Would the United States hold together without his popularity? Understandably, Washington reminded his audience that they had adopted a good Constitution, which would continue to attract their loyalty no matter who was in office.

Towards the preservation of your government, and the permanency of your present happy state, it is requisite, not only that you steadily discountenance irregular oppositions to

> its acknowledged authority, but also that you resist with care
> the spirit of innovation upon its principles, however specious
> the pretexts.

The new government had to deal with opposition to its authority, but Washington warned that changing the Constitution through amendments or expanding the government would be just as problematic as opposing it altogether.

> The alternate domination of one faction over another, sharpened by the spirit of revenge, natural to party dissension, which in different ages and countries has perpetrated the most horrid enormities, is itself a frightful despotism. But this leads at length to a more formal and permanent despotism. The disorders and miseries, which result, gradually incline the minds of men to seek security and repose in the absolute power of an individual; and sooner or later the chief of some prevailing faction, more able or more fortunate than his competitors, turns this disposition to the purposes of his own elevation, on the ruins of Public Liberty.

What President Washington is saying here is that no one is really free when there is no peace. Thus, conflicts can eventually make people susceptible to elevating someone to a power position simply because he could defeat all other factions and provide peace—even if done at the expense of liberty. Washington was troubled by this notion and issued a strong warning against this.

★   ★   ★

The necessity of reciprocal checks in the exercise of political power, by dividing and distributing it into different depositories, and constituting each the Guardian of the Public Weal against invasions by the others, has been evinced by experiments ancient and modern; some of them in our country and under our own eyes. To preserve them must be as necessary as to institute them.

President Washington spoke as one convinced that simply establishing the government was not enough—that everyone in future generations must work to preserve that government. This would require continual education about why the government is structured as it is and the training to act in a way that reinforces the balance of power codified in the Constitution. A balance of political powers would take as much effort to maintain as it did to create.

18

As a very important source of strength and security, cherish public credit.
—GEORGE WASHINGTON

President George Washington's Farewell Address, Part Two, September 17, 1796

Of all the dispositions and habits, which lead to political prosperity, Religion and Morality are indispensable supports. In vain would that man claim the tribute of Patriotism, who should labor to subvert these great pillars of human happiness, these firmest props of the duties of Men and Citizens. The mere Politician, equally with the pious man, ought to respect and to cherish them. A volume could not trace all their connexions with private and public felicity. Let it simply be asked, Where is the security for property, for reputation, for life, if the sense of religious obligation desert the oaths, which are the instruments of investigation in Courts of Justice? And let us with caution indulge the supposition, that morality can be maintained without religion. Whatever may be conceded to the influence of refined education on minds of peculiar structure, reason and experience both forbid us to expect, that national morality can prevail in exclusion of religious principle.

The French Revolution had started seven years earlier. From those years of bloodshed, President Washington had gained a great deal of information about what happens when a movement demands the elimination of religious belief. While the Constitution provides some religious constraint, many, including Washington, believed that it could only work as a stable government if the people were internally constrained by a conscience, which was based on a "fear of God."

Promote, then, as an object of primary importance, institutions for the general diffusion of knowledge. In proportion as the structure of a government gives force to public opinion, it is essential that public opinion should be enlightened.

President Washington believed the newly formed United States was only as good as its citizens. The Constitution provided the country with many protections, but there was no protection from widespread ignorance among voters. He, therefore, urged that education was to be a top priority for all people.

As a very important source of strength and security, cherish public credit. One method of preserving it is, to use it as sparingly as possible; avoiding occasions of expense by cultivating peace, but remembering also that timely disbursements to prepare for danger frequently prevent much greater disbursements to repel it; avoiding likewise the accumulation of debt, not only by shunning occasions of expense, but by vigorous exertions in time of peace to discharge the debts, which unavoidable wars may have occasioned, not ungenerously throwing upon posterity the burthen, which we ourselves ought to bear. The execution of these maxims belongs to your representatives, but it is necessary that public opinion should cooperate. To facilitate to them the performance of their duty, it is essential that you should practically bear in mind, that towards the payment of debts there must be Revenue; that to have Revenue there must be taxes; that no taxes can be devised, which are not more or less inconvenient and unpleasant; that the intrinsic embarrassment, inseparable from the selection of the proper objects (which is always a choice of difficulties), ought to be a decisive motive for a candid construction of the conduct of the government in making it, and for a spirit of acquiescence in the measures for obtaining revenue, which the public exigencies may at any time dictate.

The Founders believed debt was never a good thing. Certainly, debt is unavoidable when a country goes to war, but the Founders believed that in peacetime debt needed to be paid off as quickly as possible. The Founders also knew that Americans had a strong distaste for taxes. After all, it was over the issue of taxation that the colonists went to war against Britain seeking independence. President Washington gently reminded Americans that taxes are inevitable and even necessary for the strength of the country, but he issued a stronger warning and admonition—to Congress, no doubt—that government spending must be kept as low as possible to avoid debt and the need for raising taxes.

> In the execution of such a plan, nothing is more essential, than that permanent, inveterate antipathies against particular Nations, and passionate attachments for others, should be excluded; and that, in place of them, just and amicable feelings towards all should be cultivated. The Nation, which indulges towards another an habitual hatred, or an habitual fondness, is in some degree a slave. It is a slave to its animosity or to its affection, either of which is sufficient to lead it astray from its duty and its interest.

Here, Washington is stating that decisions about America's defense must be based on rational evidence of what was in the nation's best interest. He also says that emotional attachment to one nation—or hatred of another—should never be a factor in international relations.

> As avenues to foreign influence in innumerable ways, such attachments are particularly alarming to the truly enlightened and independent Patriot. How many opportunities do they afford to tamper with domestic factions, to practise the arts of seduction, to mislead public opinion, to influence or awe the Public Councils! Such an attachment of a small or weak, towards a great and powerful nation, dooms the former to be the satellite of the latter.

Against the insidious wiles of foreign influence (I conjure you to believe me, fellow-citizens,) the jealousy of a free people ought to be constantly awake; since history and experience prove, that foreign influence is one of the most baneful foes of Republican Government.

Washington knew that foreign nations would use lobbyists and money to influence the American press, politicians, and policies for their own purposes—even if those purposes were not in the best interests of the American people. It was necessary for citizens to become educated and watchful regarding these hidden and dangerous influences. Otherwise, America would be destined to become a satellite of, or slave to, a stronger foreign power.

Our detached and distant situation invites and enables us to pursue a different course. If we remain one people, under an efficient government, the period is not far off, when we may defy material injury from external annoyance; when we may take such an attitude as will cause the neutrality, we may at any time resolve upon, to be scrupulously respected; when belligerent nations, under the impossibility of making acquisitions upon us, will not lightly hazard the giving us provocation; when we may choose peace or war, as our interest, guided by justice, shall counsel.

President Washington was aware of how European politics worked when small nations shared borders and engaged in conflicts with one another. The United States had the special advantage of being geographically isolated from most of the world. Washington wanted Americans to realize this unique situation, and learn how to take advantage of it. If America could remain neutral during the critical early stages of existence, Washington believed she would grow strong and formidable, and by maintaining this neutrality other nations would think twice before attacking the United States.

19

Soldiers, Sailors, and Airmen of the Allied Expeditionary Force! You are about to embark upon the Great Crusade, toward which we have striven these many months. The eyes of the world are upon you. The hope and prayers of liberty-loving people everywhere march with you.
—General Dwight D. Eisenhower

President Franklin Delano Roosevelt's 'Infamy Speech,' December 8, 1941

On December 7, 1941, the Japanese launched a premeditated and devastating attack on the U.S. naval base at Pearl Harbor, Hawaii. The next day, at 12:30 PM and before a joint session of Congress, President Roosevelt delivered his famous "Infamy Speech." Shortly after the speech, Congress formally declared war on Japan, and the U.S. was officially engaged in World War II.

★   ★   ★

Yesterday, December 7, 1941–a date which will live in infamy–the United States of America was suddenly and deliberately attacked by naval and air forces of the Empire of Japan.

The United States was at peace with that nation and, at the solicitation of Japan, was still in conversation with its Government and its Emperor looking toward the maintenance of peace in the Pacific.

If Japan had not launched an unprovoked attack at Pearl Harbor, it was unlikely the United States would have entered World War II. Most Americans remembered too clearly the devastation of World War I and were not eager to become involved in another war. Japan, as an ally of Germany and Italy, provoked America to go to war by the attack.

It will be recorded that the distance of Hawaii from Japan makes it obvious that the attack was deliberately planned many days or even weeks ago. During the intervening time the Japanese Government has deliberately sought to deceive the United States by false statements and expressions of hope for continued peace.

The attack yesterday on the Hawaiian Islands has caused severe damage to American naval and military forces. Very many American lives have been lost. In addition American ships have been reported torpedoed on the high seas between San Francisco and Honolulu.

The attack on Pearl Harbor resulted in the loss of nearly 2,400 lives— almost two-thirds of these deaths within the first 15 minutes of the initial assault. But what made the attack even more malicious was that the Japanese—while planning this deadly attack—had deliberately led the Americans to believe they wanted peace. At the time, America was a peace-seeking nation, and Japan had deliberately taken advantage of America's good will.

Japan has, therefore, undertaken a surprise offensive extending throughout the Pacific area. The facts of yesterday speak for themselves. The people of the United States have already formed their opinions and well understand the implications to the very life and safety of our nation.

As Commander-in-Chief of the Army and Navy, I have directed that all measures be taken for our defense.

Always will we remember the character of the onslaught against us. No matter how long it may take us to overcome this premeditated invasion, the American people in their righteous might will win through to absolute victory.

I believe I interpret the will of the Congress and of the people when I assert that we will not only defend ourselves to the uttermost but will make very certain that this form of treachery shall never endanger us again.

President Roosevelt expressed a sentiment that resonated with America's heritage: that we had never tolerated an aggressor nation to threaten America's way of life or security. Not only was Roosevelt resolved to defeat Japan, but the attack on Pearl Harbor was reason to rethink American defensive policy so that the United States would never be vulnerable to such an attack again.

★　　★　　★

Hostilities exist. There is no blinking at the fact that our people, our territory and our interests are in grave danger.

With confidence in our armed forces—with the unbounded determination of our people—we will gain the inevitable triumph—so help us God.

I ask that the Congress declare that since the unprovoked and dastardly attack by Japan on Sunday, December seventh, a state of war has existed between the United States and the Japanese Empire."

President Roosevelt reiterated an important American quality. Although the United States has never been a war-loving nation, when she is threatened or attacked, America's intention has always been to defend herself until the "inevitable triumph" has been accomplished.

★　　★　　★

General Dwight D. Eisenhower's 'Order of the Day,' June 6, 1944

June 6, 1944—D-Day—is one of the most famous days in world history. On that day, the largest amphibious assault ever launched was thrust against the Germans by the Allies (the "big three" being the US, Great Britain and the Soviet Union) in Normandy, France. Over 176,000 men, 20,000 vehicles, and thousands of tons of weapons left the coast of England for Normandy. Just prior to the start of the assault, General Dwight Eisenhower, the Supreme Commander of the Allied Expeditionary Forces, issued his "Order of the Day." It is one of the most moving and powerful rally cries ever issued.

Supreme Headquarters Allied Expeditionary Force
Soldiers, Sailors, and Airmen of the Allied Expeditionary Force!

You are about to embark upon the Great Crusade, toward which we have striven these many months. The eyes of the world are upon you. The hope and prayers of liberty-loving people everywhere march with you. In company with our brave Allies and brothers-in-arms on other Fronts, you will bring about the destruction of the German war machine, the elimination of Nazi tyranny over the oppressed peoples of Europe, and security for ourselves in a free world.

Eisenhower's "Order of the Day" made it clear that the war in Europe was an extension of the principles fought for in the Revolutionary War. The signers of the Declaration of Independence had fought to liberate their land from a dominating power. The soldiers of the Allied Expeditionary Force were fighting tyranny, ending oppression, and establishing a secure future for the United States and other nations.

Your task will not be an easy one. Your enemy is well trained, well equipped and battle-hardened. He will fight savagely.

There had been German losses in North Africa, Italy and Russia, including German losses in air and naval forces. Nevertheless, Germany still held a stronghold on Europe. German soldiers were extremely committed to the cause for which they were fighting, and they believed passionately in Adolf Hitler. This commitment, combined with experience and training, made the Germans a formidable enemy for the Allied soldiers.

But this is the year 1944! Much has happened since the Nazi triumphs of 1940-41. The United Nations have inflicted upon the Germans great defeats, in open battle, man-to-man. Our air offensive has seriously reduced their strength in the air and their capacity to wage war on the ground. Our Home Fronts have given us an overwhelming superiority in weapons and munitions of war, and placed at our disposal great reserves of trained fighting men. The tide has turned! The free men of the world are marching together to Victory!

General Eisenhower offered encouragement to his soldiers by reminding them of some of the more recent German defeats. He also reminded the soldiers of the tremendous amount of equipment, munitions, and manpower, which fortified their assault. Eisenhower also cast an inspiring vision of the Allied soldiers as protectors of all free people in the world.

★   ★   ★

I have full confidence in your courage, devotion to duty and skill in battle. We will accept nothing less than full Victory!

Good luck! And let us beseech the blessing of Almighty God upon this great and noble undertaking.

General Eisenhower reminded his soldiers that the cause for which they were fighting was noble and mighty and he drew on his Christian background as he asked for the blessing of Almighty God.

20

*I set off upon a very good Horse; it was then about
11 o'Clock, and very pleasant . . . In Medford, I awaked
the Captain of the Minute men; and after that, I alarmed
almost every House, till I got to Lexington. . . . I likewise
mentioned, that we had better allarm all the
Inhabitents till we got to Concord.*

—PAUL REVERE

Paul Revere is one of the most recognized American patriots from
the Revolutionary War period. A successful Boston silversmith, Revere was part of the resistance movement against the British prior
to, and during, the Revolutionary War. He organized, and participated in an extensive spy network that gathered information on the
British. He is most famous for his mid-night ride in 1775 from Boston to Lexington and Concord to warn the citizens of the approach
of the British troops. In a 1798 letter to Jeremy Belknap, Revere
recounted his famous ride and the events that precipitated it.

A Letter from Paul Revere to the Corresponding Secretary, Jeremy Belknap, 1798

In the Fall of 1774 and Winter of 1775 I was one of upwards of thirty, cheifly mechanics, who formed our selves in to a Committee for the purpose of watching the Movements of the British Soldiers, and gaining every intelegence of the movements of the Tories.

The "Tories" were the colonists loyal to British rule, and they aided the British military. Long before independence had been officially declared, Britain was already sending troops to prevent the colonies from rebelling and to enforce obedience. Paul Revere was part of the underground resistance.

In the Winter, towards the Spring, we frequently took Turns, two and two, to Watch the Soldiers, By patroling the Streets all night. The Saturday Night preceding the 19th of April, about 12 oClock at Night, the Boats belonging to the Transports were all launched, and carried under the Sterns of the Men of War. (They had been previously hauld up and repaired). We likewise found that the Grenadiers and light Infantry were all taken off duty.

That the British soldiers were no longer at their regular duty indicated that they were being assigned a part in a special move. It appeared that boats were carrying these troops to the British battleships ("Men of War"). Paul Revere and his fellow watchmen detected danger.

From these movements, we expected something serious was [to] be transacted. On Tuesday evening, the 18th, it was observed, that a number of Soldiers were marching towards the bottom of the Common. About 10 o'Clock, Dr. Warren Sent in great haste for me, and beged that I would imediately Set off for Lexington, where Messrs. Hancock and Adams were, and acquaint them of the Movement, and that it was thought they were the objets.

John Hancock and Samuel Adams were two leaders of the resistance to the British attempts to add new taxes and regulations to the colonies. It appeared the British Army was preparing to take them as prisoners. If they had been captured it was virtually certain that the British would have executed them for treason. One of Paul Revere's fellow friends in the resistance movement begged him to go immediately to Lexington to warn Hancock and Adams.

I returned at Night thro Charlestown; there I agreed with a Col. Conant, and some other Gentlemen, that if the British went out by Water, we would shew two Lanthorns in the North Church Steeple; and if by Land, one, as a Signal.

Henry Wadsworth Longfellow, in his poem, "Paul Revere's Ride," portrayed the signals from the church as aimed *at* Paul Revere, rather than being signals *from* Revere. This misinformation found its way into many early history texts.

I then went Home, took my Boots and Surtout, and went

to the North part of the Town, Where I had kept a Boat; two friends rowed me across Charles River, a little to the eastward where the Somerset Man of War lay. It was then young flood, the Ship was winding, and the moon was Rising. They landed me on Charlestown side. When I got into Town, I met Col. Conant, and several others; they said they had seen our signals. I told them what was Acting, and went to git me a Horse; I got a Horse of Deacon Larkin.

The British were moving troops across the Charles River to march into Lexington and Concord, where they hoped to arrest Samuel Adams and John Hancock and confiscate weapons. Paul Revere attempted to outrun the troops, and what we see here is a comprehensive and costly network of resistors who loaned out expensive animals and risked their own safety in order to combat British power.

I set off upon a very good Horse; it was then about 11 o'Clock, and very pleasant.

This not only tells us that Paul Revere had good riding weather that helped him outrace British foot soldiers, but that his fellow patriots had provided him with a well-trained and well-bred horse. Resisting the British required generous sacrifices and the patriots willingly made those sacrifices.

> In Medford, I awaked the Captain of the Minute men; and after that, I alarmed almost every House, till I got to Lexington. I found Messrs. Hancock and Adams at the Rev. Mr. Clark's; I told them my errand,

Contrary to the popular story, Revere did not shout his message from the streets because that would have attracted the attention and the hostility of those loyal to Britain. Rather, he went and knocked on the doors of the homes of those he knew were patriots. They in turn awakened those in the area who they knew to be trustworthy. The "Minute Men" were the volunteers for the patriot militia who promised to be ready in a minute to fight British troops.

> I likewise mentioned, that we had better allarm all the Inhabitents till we got to Concord

Though Paul Revere has been given the main credit for warning of the coming British troops, there were several riders involved. Together, they warned the militia so that they could resist their British adversaries.

21

We conclude that, in the field of public education, the doctrine of 'separate but equal' has no place.
—CHIEF JUSTICE WARREN
ON BEHALF OF THE SUPREME COURT

Since 1896, when the Supreme Court decided in *Plessy v. Ferguson* that separate facilities for separate races were "equal" and not a violation of the Fourteenth Amendment's equal protection clause, racial relations in the United States had been marked by racial segregation. In 1954, in a landmark decision in *Brown v. Board of Education*, the Supreme Court unanimously overturned the "separate but equal" doctrine established by *Plessy v. Ferguson*. Many consider *Brown v. Board of Education* to be the case that launched the civil rights movement.

Brown v. Board of Education, May 17, 1954

In each of the cases, minors of the Negro race, through their legal representatives, seek the aid of the courts in obtaining admission to the public schools of their community on a non-segregated basis. In each instance, they had been denied admission to schools attended by white children under laws requiring or permitting segregation according to race. This segregation was alleged to deprive the plaintiffs of the equal protection of the laws under the Fourteenth Amendment.

The states claimed that they were submitting to the Fourteenth Amendment's mandate that blacks and whites both have equal protection under the law, even though the states required black children and white children to attend separate public schools. Blacks objected that they were not be given equal protection, but the state courts did not agree.

Today, education is perhaps the most important function of state and local governments. Compulsory school attendance laws and the great expenditures for education both demonstrate our recognition of the importance of education to our democratic society. It is required in the performance of our most basic public responsibilities, even service in the armed forces. It is the very foundation of good citizenship. Today it is a principal instrument in awakening the child to cultural values, in preparing him for later professional training, and in helping him to adjust normally to his environment. In these days, it is doubtful that any child may reasonably be expected to succeed in life if he is denied the opportunity of an education. Such an opportunity, where the state has undertaken to provide it, is a right which must be made available to all on equal terms.

The Supreme Court affirmed a belief that Americans have held dear since the days of George Washington: that education should be one of the most important priorities of any country because it is the very foundation of a strong citizenry and nation. The court said that when states assume the great responsibility of providing public education, they couldn't treat groups of citizens differently.

We come then to the question presented: Does segregation of children in public schools solely on the basis of race, even though the physical facilities and other "tangible" factors may be equal, deprive the children of the minority group of equal educational opportunities? We believe that it does.

The court bypassed arguments about whether or not the separate educations of whites and blacks were equal by deciding that segregating children on the basis of race is inherently unequal and places an unjust burden on minorities.

Segregation of white and colored children in public schools has a detrimental effect upon the colored children. The impact is greater when it has the sanction of the law, for the policy of separating the races is usually interpreted as denoting the inferiority of the negro group. A sense of inferiority affects the motivation of a child to learn. Segregation with the sanction of law, therefore, has a tendency to [retard] the educational and mental development of negro children and to deprive them of some of the benefits they would receive in a racial[ly] integrated school system.

The court had already stated that segregation based on race is inherently unequal, but here the court pointed out that the negative effects of segregation are made much worse when sanctioned by the government authorities. Black children are led to believe that they are inferior, which deprives them of a motivation to learn and succeed.

Whatever may have been the extent of psychological knowledge at the time of Plessy v. Ferguson, this finding is amply supported by modern authority. Any language in Plessy v. Ferguson contrary to this finding is rejected.

Plessy v. Ferguson was the landmark Supreme Court ruling in 1896 that established that the "separate but equal" accommodation for blacks and whites was constitutional. The ruling was mainly about passenger railroad trains, but it was also applied to education. In the *Brown v. Board of Education* decision, the Supreme Court firmly rejected the belief that separate can still be equal.

We conclude that, in the field of public education, the doctrine of "separate but equal" has no place. Separate educational facilities are inherently unequal. Therefore, we hold that the plaintiffs and others similarly situated for whom the actions have been brought are, by reason of the segregation complained of, deprived of the equal protection of the laws guaranteed by the Fourteenth Amendment. This disposition makes unnecessary any discussion whether such segregation also violates the Due Process Clause of the Fourteenth Amendment.

The Fourteenth Amendment guarantees "equal protection" for every American citizen under the law and also an equal right to "due process" if a person thinks they have been deprived of any right. The lawyers for the black students claimed segregation violated both clauses. The Supreme Court found that segregation violated the "equal protection" clause of the Fourteenth Amendment and, because they overturned the law based on the violation of "equal protection," felt no need discuss the implications of the "due process" clause. The state and federal governments have to provide one education for all races.

22

> *We owe it, therefore, to candor and to the amicable relations existing between the United States and those (European) powers to declare that we should consider any attempt on their part to extend their system to any portion of this hemisphere as dangerous to our peace and safety.*
> —JAMES MONROE

In 1823, several Latin American countries were on the verge of becoming independent of Spain. The United States, headed by President James Monroe, was concerned that other European powers might try to colonize the newly independent countries. To ward off this intervention and warn those Old World powers that the New World—the Americas—were off limits to their colonization, Monroe issued what is now known as the Monroe Doctrine during his State of the Union address before Congress. The Monroe Doctrine remains the most influential and profound statement of U.S. foreign policy and has been invoked by numerous presidents in the generations since 1823.

The Monroe Doctrine, December 2, 1823

In the discussions to which this interest has given rise and in the arrangements by which they may terminate the occasion has been judged proper for asserting, as a principle in which the rights and interests of the United States are involved, that the American continents, by the free and independent condition which they have assumed and maintain, are henceforth not to be considered as subjects for future colonization by any European powers. . .

As George Washington had hoped, the U.S. had grown to the point that it was taken seriously by European powers. After even winning independence from Britain, the United States continually had to deal with European nations attempting to expand their colonies and influence in the Americas. President Monroe declared that the United States wanted no more European expansion into the Americas.

In the wars of the European powers in matters relating to themselves we have never taken any part, nor does it comport with our policy to do so. It is only when our rights are invaded or seriously menaced that we resent injuries or make preparation for our defense. With the movements in this hemisphere we are of necessity more immediately connected, and by causes which must be obvious to all enlightened and impartial observers. The political system of the allied powers is essentially different in this respect from that of America. This difference proceeds from that which exists in their respective Governments; and to the defense of our own, which has been achieved by the loss of so much blood and treasure, and matured by the wisdom of their most enlightened citizens, and under which we have enjoyed unexampled felicity, this whole nation is devoted. We owe it, therefore, to candor and to the amicable relations existing between the United States and those powers to declare that we should consider any attempt on their part to extend their system to any portion of this hemisphere as dangerous to our peace and safety.

America had refused to get involved in European affairs and Monroe insisted that Europe do the same for the American continents. Since the United States was a republic and committed to republican principles, Monroe believed that it would be threatening to U.S. interests to have monarchies extend into North or South America.

Our policy in regard to Europe, which was adopted at an early stage of the wars which have so long agitated that quarter of the globe, nevertheless remains the same, which is, not to interfere in the internal concerns of any of its powers; to consider the government de facto as the legitimate government for us; to cultivate friendly relations with it, and to preserve those relations by a frank, firm, and manly policy, meeting in all instances the just claims of every power, submitting to injuries from none. But in regard to those continents circumstances are eminently and conspicuously different. It is impossible that the allied powers should extend their political system to any portion of either continent without endangering our peace and happiness; nor can anyone believe that our southern brethren, if left to themselves, would adopt it of their own accord. It is equally impossible, therefore, that we should behold such interposition in any form with indifference.

While Monroe wanted to remain friends and allies with all European nations, he believed it was important for the American continents to be a safe-haven for republican governments. If European rulers attempted to extend their authority into the Americas, the U.S. would regard it as a threat to its national interest.

It is still the true policy of the United States to leave the parties to themselves, in hope that other powers will pursue the same course.

The isolationist point of view was a critical part of the Monroe Doctrine. President Monroe stressed repeatedly that the United States' foreign policy was to leave other powers to themselves, and he offered a veiled warning in his request that other nations extend the same courtesy, respect or consideration to the American continents: "In the wars of the European powers, in matters relating to themselves, we have never taken part, nor does it comport with our policy, so to do."

23

> *Thus, the particular phraseology of the constitution of the United States confirms and strengthens the principle . . . that a law repugnant to the constitution is void; and that courts, as well as other departments, are bound by that instrument.*
> —CHIEF JUSTICE MARSHALL
> ON BEHALF OF THE SUPREME COURT

Marbury v. Madison was a landmark Supreme Court decision that helped solidify the system of checks and balances established by the Founding Fathers in the U.S. Constitution. This case, argued over the commission of William Marbury as Justice of the Peace in Washington DC, established "judicial review" an important concept that gives authority to the courts to oversee and overturn the actions of other branches of government. The decision in *Marbury v. Madison*, which was the first time the Supreme Court declared something unconstitutional, shapes the way our judicial system operates today.

Marbury v. Madison, February 24, 1803

The very essence of civil liberty certainly consists in the right of every individual to claim the protection of the laws, whenever he receives an injury. One of the first duties of government is to afford that protection. [The] government of the United States has been emphatically termed a government of laws, and not of men. It will certainly cease to deserve this high appellation, if the laws furnish no remedy for the violation of a vested legal right. . . .

The Supreme Court argued that it has the right and duty to consider whether laws passed by Congress are constitutional. They further argued that the rule of law could not last if Congress could pass laws that are in violation of the Constitution.

In the distribution of this power it is declared that "the Supreme Court shall have original jurisdiction in all cases affecting ambassadors, other public ministers and consuls, and those in which a state shall be a party. In all other cases, the Supreme Court shall have appellate jurisdiction."

In this clause, it is clear that in a nation ruled by laws, the exact words of the United States Constitution are extremely important. What the document actually says must be honored as the basis for all arguments about the law.

That the people have an original right to establish, for their future government, such principles as, in their opinion, shall most conduce to their own happiness, is the basis on which the whole American fabric has been erected. The exercise of this original right is a very great exertion; nor can it, nor ought it, to be frequently repeated. The principles, therefore, so established, are deemed fundamental. And as the authority from which they proceed is supreme, and can seldom act, they are designed to be permanent.

Here, the Supreme Court pointed out that the people did not establish the Constitution in order to have to establish it again and again every time Congress assembled. If Congress can pass unconstitutional laws then they are essentially making a new Constitution every time they pass such laws. This defeats the purpose of establishing the Constitution in the first place.

The powers of the legislature are defined and limited; and that those limits may not be mistaken, or forgotten, the constitution is written. To what purpose are powers limited, and to what purpose is that limitation committed to writing, if these limits may, at any time, be passed by those intended to be restrained? The distinction between a government with limited and unlimited powers is abolished, if those limits do not confine the persons on whom they are imposed, and if acts prohibited and acts allowed, are of equal obligation. It is a proposition too plain to be contested, that the constitution controls any legislative act repugnant to it; or, that the legislature may alter the constitution by an ordinary act.

Between these alternatives there is no middle ground. The constitution is either a superior, paramount law, unchangeable by ordinary means, or it is on a level with ordinary legislative acts, and, like other acts, is alterable when the legislature shall please to alter it.

If the former part of the alternative be true, then a legislative act contrary to the constitution is not law: if the latter part be true, then written constitutions are absurd attempts, on the part of the people, to limit a power in its own nature illimitable.

This provision is quite simple: either we have a Constitution that is the supreme law of the land and which Congress is accountable to, or else we have no Constitution at all.

Certainly all those who have framed written constitutions contemplate them as forming the fundamental and paramount law of the nation, and consequently, the theory of every such government must be, that an act of the legislature, repugnant to the constitution, is void.

This theory is essentially attached to a written constitution, and is, consequently, to be considered, by this court, as one of the fundamental principles of our society. It is not therefore to be lost sight of in the further consideration of this subject.

Notice that to be ruled by a fundamental law—i.e., the Constitution—granting specific powers to the government is considered "one of the fundamental principles of our society." Whether or not an act of government is constitutional can never be mocked as an unimportant question.

It is emphatically the province and duty of the judicial department to say what the law is. Those who apply the rule to particular cases, must of necessity expound and interpret that rule. If two laws conflict with each other, the courts must decide on the operation of each.

The Supreme Court argued that if the Constitution is the law of the land, then the judicial branch of the government must be responsible for determining whether or not the laws of Congress are in conflict with the Constitution. Here the Supreme Court firmly established the concept of judicial review.

If, then, the courts are to regard the constitution, and the constitution is superior to any ordinary act of the legislature, the constitution, and not such ordinary act, must govern the case to which they both apply.

In other words, when there is a law passed by Congress that conflicts with what the Constitution says, then the Constitution wins and Congress loses.

The judicial power of the United States is extended to all cases arising under the constitution.

> Could it be the intention of those who gave this power, to say
> that in using it the constitution should not be looked into?
> That a case arising under the constitution should be decided
> without examining the instrument under which it arises?
>
> This is too extravagant to be maintained.

This decision states that it is absurd to think that the highest court
in the judicial branch would not be concerned with what the Constitution says. That notion defies logic and renders the Constitution moot and/or impotent.

24

With malice toward none; with charity for all;
with firmness in the right, as God gives us to see
the right, let us strive on to finish the work we are in;
to bind up the nation's wounds; to care for him who
shall have borne the battle, and for his widow,
and his orphan — to do all which may achieve
and cherish, a just and a lasting peace, among
ourselves, and with all nations.
—ABRAHAM LINCOLN

When Abraham Lincoln delivered his second inaugural address on March 4, 1865, the Civil War was nearing its end and much of the focus of the Union was on Reconstruction. Lincoln's address was not one of a victorious leader on the verge of defeating a foe. Instead, it reflected sadness at the losses the nation had experienced during the previous four years of warfare. Some experts believe Lincoln used this address to defend his approach to Reconstruction, which avoided a harsh treatment of the South, because in the speech he reminded listeners that blame lay with both sides during the war. Despite the sad tone of the speech, Lincoln ended with a hopeful charge to his fellow countrymen that they forgive and heal the wounds of the past and move forward as a stronger Union.

President Abraham Lincoln's Second Inaugural Address, March 4, 1865

Fellow-Countrymen: At this second appearing to take the oath of the Presidential office there is less occasion for an extended address than there was at the first. Then a statement somewhat in detail of a course to be pursued seemed fitting and proper. Now, at the expiration of four years, during which public declarations have been constantly called forth on every point and phase of the great contest which still absorbs the attention and engrosses the energies of the nation, little that is new could be presented. The progress of our arms, upon which all else chiefly depends, is as well known to the public as to myself, and it is, I trust, reasonably satisfactory and encouraging to all. With high hope for the future, no prediction in regard to it is ventured.

Lincoln began his address by stating that since the events of his first term—chiefly, the Civil War—had consumed the thoughts and attentions of the country, there was little he could say that would be new.

On the occasion corresponding to this four years ago all thoughts were anxiously directed to an impending civil war. All dreaded it, all sought to avert it. While the inaugural

address was being delivered from this place, devoted
altogether to saving the Union without war, insurgent agents
were in the city seeking to destroy it without war—seeking
to dissolve the Union and divide effects by negotiation.
Both parties deprecated war, but one of them would make
war rather than let the nation survive, and the other would
accept war rather than let it perish, and the war came.

Lincoln reminded his listeners that war was never his objective
that, in fact, he sought to avoid it at all costs. But he didn't lay full
blame on any one party for the war. He said that while one region
provoked war, the other was more than happy to accept it in order
to save the Union.

One-eighth of the whole population were colored slaves,
not distributed generally over the Union, but localized in
the southern part of it. These slaves constituted a peculiar
and powerful interest. All knew that this interest was
somehow the cause of the war. To strengthen, perpetuate,
and extend this interest was the object for which the
insurgents would rend the Union even by war, while the
Government claimed no right to do more than to restrict
the territorial enlargement of it. Neither party expected for
the war the magnitude or the duration which it has already
attained. Neither anticipated that the cause of the conflict
might cease with or even before the conflict itself should
cease. Each looked for an easier triumph, and a result less
fundamental and astounding. Both read the same Bible and
pray to the same God, and each invokes His aid against the

other. It may seem strange that any men should dare to ask a just God's assistance in wringing their bread from the sweat of other men's faces, but let us judge not, that we be not judged. The prayers of both could not be answered. That of neither has been answered fully. The Almighty has His own purposes. "Woe unto the world because of offenses; for it must needs be that offenses come, but woe to that man by whom the offense cometh." If we shall suppose that American slavery is one of those offenses which, in the providence of God, must needs come, but which, having continued through His appointed time, He now wills to remove, and that He gives to both North and South this terrible war as the woe due to those by whom the offense came, shall we discern therein any departure from those divine attributes which the believers in a living God always ascribe to Him? Fondly do we hope, fervently do we pray, that this mighty scourge of war may speedily pass away. Yet, if God wills that it continue until all the wealth piled by the bondsman's two hundred and fifty years of unrequited toil shall be sunk, and until every drop of blood drawn with the lash shall be paid by another drawn with the sword, as was said three thousand years ago, so still it must be said "the judgments of the Lord are true and righteous altogether."

This section of the speech is powerful and humbling. Lincoln reminded listeners that opponents in the Civil War both read the same Bible and prayed to the same God, and that neither anticipated a war as long and devastating as this war had been.

Lincoln made several biblical references in this section, which reflected his own faith. Most notable is his statement that "the Almighty has His own purposes." In other words, it's not for men to know the will of God. This statement was controversial in Lincoln's time, because both sides in the Civil War believed firmly that the will of God was for their side to achieve victory over the other.

> With malice toward none, with charity for all, with firmness in the right as God gives us to see the right, let us strive on to finish the work we are in, to bind up the nation's wounds, to care for him who shall have borne the battle and for his widow and his orphan, to do all which may achieve and cherish a just and lasting peace among ourselves and with all nations.

Lincoln finished his address by encouraging all Americans to heal the wounds of the war, care for their fellow citizen—whether from the North or the South—and seek a lasting peace with each other and the rest of the world. This statement is one of the most poetic and beautiful in all of Lincoln's oratory.

The *London Spectator* declared Lincoln's message to be "the noblest political document known to history."

25

No free government can stand without virtue in
the people and a lofty spirit of patriotism, and if
the sordid feelings of mere selfishness shall usurp
the place which ought to be filled by public spirit,
the legislation of Congress will soon be converted into
a scramble for personal and sectional advantages.
—ANDREW JACKSON

Andrew Jackson was a native of Tennessee and the seventh president of the United States. His political philosophy was marked by expanding political participation to more of the citizenry, expanding the geography of America westward—under the philosophy of "Manifest Destiny"—a hands-off approach to the economy, protection of states rights, and expanding the powers of the executive branch. Nicknamed "Old Hickory" for his toughness, Jackson was a war hero from the War of 1812 and was most renowned for his command of American forces in the Battle of New Orleans. He delivered his farewell address on March 4, 1837 after two terms as president.

President Andrew Jackson's
Farewell Address, March 4, 1837

In the legislation of Congress also, and in every measure of the General Government, justice to every portion of the United States should be faithfully observed. No free government can stand without virtue in the people and a lofty spirit of patriotism, and if the sordid feelings of mere selfishness shall usurp the place which ought to be filled by public spirit, the legislation of Congress will soon be converted into a scramble for personal and sectional advantages. Under our free institutions the citizens of every quarter of our country are capable of attaining a high degree of prosperity and happiness without seeking to profit themselves at the expense of others; and every such attempt must in the end fail to succeed, for the people in every part of the United States are too enlightened not to understand their own rights and interests and to detect and defeat every effort to gain undue advantages over them; and when such designs are discovered it naturally provokes resentments which can not always be easily allayed. Justice—full and ample justice to every portion of the United States should be the ruling principle of every freeman, and should guide the deliberations of every public body, whether it be State or national.

If everyone tries to live at the expense of everyone else, the only result can be mass poverty. The only people who "prosper" in such circumstances will be the politicians who gain office by promising their voters they will plunder others for their benefit. President Jackson begged the American people to seek impartial justice—not special favors—from their government. Freedom allows people everywhere to prosper without taking prosperity away from others.

It is well known that there have always been those amongst us who wish to enlarge the powers of the General Government, and experience would seem to indicate that there is a tendency on the part of this Government to overstep the boundaries marked out for it by the Constitution. Its legitimate authority is abundantly sufficient for all the purposes for which it was created, and its powers being expressly enumerated, there can be no justification for claiming anything beyond them. Every attempt to exercise power beyond these limits should be promptly and firmly opposed, for one evil example will lead to other measures still more mischievous; and if the principle of constructive powers or supposed advantages or temporary circumstances shall ever be permitted to justify the assumption of a power not given by the Constitution, the General Government will before long absorb all the powers of legislation, and you will have in effect but one consolidated government. From the extent of our country, its diversified interests, different pursuits, and different habits, it is too obvious for argument that a single consolidated government would be wholly inadequate to watch over and protect its interests; and every friend of our free institutions should be always prepared to maintain unimpaired and in full vigor the rights and sovereignty of the States and to confine the action of the General Government strictly to the sphere of its appropriate duties.

Jackson wanted the federal government to be limited to the very specific powers granted to it by the Constitution. He argued that any exception to that rule would produce more and more exceptions until the federal government took over all the authority and responsibilities of the state governments. He thought it was obvious that a country so large could not be efficiently governed from Washington DC. The state governments needed to keep their powers and responsibilities because each was better able to deal with the interests and needs of their own people.

There is, perhaps, no one of the powers conferred on the Federal Government so liable to abuse as the taxing power. The most productive and convenient sources of revenue were necessarily given to it, that it might be able to perform the important duties imposed upon it; and the taxes which it lays upon commerce being concealed from the real payer in the price of the article, they do not so readily attract the attention of the people as smaller sums demanded from them directly by the taxgatherer. But the tax imposed on goods enhances by so much the price of the commodity to the consumer, and as many of these duties are imposed on articles of necessity which are daily used by the great body of the people, the money raised by these imposts is drawn from their pockets. Congress has no right under the Constitution to take money from the people unless it is required to execute some one of the specific powers intrusted to the Government; and if they raise more than is

> necessary for such purposes, it is an abuse of the power of
> taxation, and unjust and oppressive.

Taxes on imports in Jackson's day were largely hidden from the consumer. But they still took money from the consumer. Jackson laid down two rules: (1) taxes should only go to fund legitimate and constitutional government activities; and (2) taxes should only be for the amount necessary for those activities. Any taxation over that amount is an injustice.

> It is unquestionably our true interest to cultivate the most
> friendly understanding with every nation and to avoid by
> every honorable means the calamities of war, and we shall
> best attain this object by frankness and sincerity in our
> foreign intercourse, by the prompt and faithful execution of
> treaties, and by justice and impartiality in our conduct to all.
> But no nation, however desirous of peace, can hope to escape
> occasional collisions with other powers, and the soundest
> dictates of policy require that we should place ourselves in a
> condition to assert our rights if a resort to force should ever
> become necessary.

Jackson wanted peace but he was also realistic about the need to be prepared when armed conflict was unavoidable. Here, he was pointing out that the U.S. government must be prepared when such conflicts arise.

26

The men of Normandy had faith that what they were doing was right, faith that they fought for all humanity, faith that a just God would grant them mercy on this beachhead, or on the next. It was the deep knowledge— and pray God we have not lost it—that there is a profound moral difference between the use of force for liberation and the use of force for conquest.
—RONALD REAGAN

On June 6, 1984, Ronald Reagan stood before an audience of civilians and veterans at Point Du Hoc, Normandy, France, where, forty years before, brave U.S. Army Rangers ascended a sheer cliff under fire from German machine guns to free France and much of Europe from German oppression. He delivered a speech that honored the memory of those who sacrificed their lives for freedom and exhorted all lovers of freedom to persist in pursuing it, no matter the cost.

President Ronald Reagan's Remarks on the 40th Anniversary of D-Day, June 6, 1984

We're here to mark that day in history when the Allied armies joined in battle to reclaim this continent to liberty. For four long years, much of Europe had been under a terrible shadow. Free nations had fallen, Jews cried out in the camps, millions cried out for liberation. Europe was enslaved and the world prayed for its rescue. Here, in Normandy, the rescue began. Here, the Allies stood and fought against tyranny, in a giant undertaking unparalleled in human history.

We stand on a lonely, windswept point on the northern shore of France. The air is soft, but forty years ago at this moment, the air was dense with smoke and the cries of men, and the air was filled with the crack of rifle fire and the roar of cannon. At dawn, on the morning of the 6th of June, 1944, two hundred and twenty-five Rangers jumped off the British landing craft and ran to the bottom of these cliffs.

Their mission was one of the most difficult and daring of the invasion: to climb these sheer and desolate cliffs and take out the enemy guns. The Allies had been told that some of the mightiest of these guns were here, and they would be trained on the beaches to stop the Allied advance.

The Rangers looked up and saw the enemy soldiers at the edge of the cliffs, shooting down at them with machine guns and throwing grenades. And the American Rangers began to climb. They shot rope ladders over the face of these cliffs and began to pull themselves up. When one Ranger fell, another would take his place. When one rope was cut, a Ranger would grab another and begin his climb again. They climbed, shot back, and held their footing. Soon, one by one, the Rangers pulled themselves over the top, and in seizing the firm land at the top of these cliffs, they began to seize back the continent of Europe. Two hundred and twenty-five came here. After two days of fighting, only ninety could still bear arms.

By describing the great sacrifices made by the Rangers on D-Day, Reagan showed that the battle for independence and freedom is a worldwide, timeless battle. In 1944, the whole of Europe was groaning under a vicious tyranny. The United States could have easily stayed out of the European war that, until Pearl Harbor, was not their fight. But, ultimately, when it was clear and undeniable that the fundamental issue of freedom was at stake, American soldiers traveled far from home to fight for the liberty of other nations.

The United States was willing to pay dearly for the liberty of others, as evidenced by the blood of America's own young men, like the Rangers who climbed Point Du Hoc on D-Day.

The men of Normandy had faith that what they were doing was right, faith that they fought for all humanity, faith that a just God would grant them mercy on this beachhead, or on the next. It was the deep knowledge – and pray God we have not lost it – that there is a profound moral difference between the use of force for liberation and the use of force for conquest. You were here to liberate, not to conquer, and

so you and those others did not doubt your cause. And you were right not to doubt.

President Reagan addressed the cynicism that claims that all military operations are equally evil. Such a view looks at all use of armed force by governments as a form of oppression. Forty years after D-Day some critics were using such a perspective to oppose Reagan's own stance against the Soviet Union. But the principles of the Declaration of Independence insist that people use force to help other people win liberty from tyrants. Reagan restated those principles by showing how they were at work on D-Day.

You all knew that some things are worth dying for. One's country is worth dying for, and democracy is worth dying for, because it's the most deeply honorable form of government ever devised by man. All of you loved liberty. All of you were willing to fight tyranny, and you knew the people of your countries were behind you.

The Americans who fought here that morning knew word of the invasion was spreading through the darkness back home. They fought – or felt in their hearts, though they couldn't know in fact, that in Georgia they were filling the churches at 4:00 am. In Kansas they were kneeling on their porches and praying. And in Philadelphia they were ringing the Liberty Bell.

Something else helped the men of D-day; their rock-hard belief that Providence would have a great hand in the events that would unfold here; that God was an ally in this great

cause. And so, the night before the invasion, when Colonel Wolverton asked his parachute troops to kneel with him in prayer, he told them: "Do not bow your heads, but look up so you can see God and ask His blessing in what we're about to do." Also, that night, General Matthew Ridgway on his cot, listening in the darkness for the promise God made to Joshua: "I will not fail thee nor forsake thee."

President Reagan spoke directly to veterans from that military operation forty years earlier. Just as Patrick Henry promised that Providence would judge the cause of freedom and aid the colonists against Britain, in 1944 the same reliance was invoked. The ringing of the Liberty Bell, the prayers of the faithful in churches, and the prayers of military officers all showed that the fight for liberty in Normandy was an extension of the same fight in 1776. The confidence of the Founders in a just God who rules the nations and works justice, was still alive in 1944.

We're bound today by what bound us 40 years ago, the same loyalties, traditions, and beliefs. We're bound by reality. The strength of America's allies is vital to the United States, and the American security guarantee is essential to the continued freedom of Europe's democracies. We were with you then; we're with you now. Your hopes are our hopes, and your destiny is our destiny.

Here, in this place where the West held together, let us make a vow to our dead. Let us show them by our actions that we understand what they died for. Let our actions say to them the words for which Matthew Ridgway listened: "I will not fail thee nor forsake thee."

Strengthened by their courage and heartened by their value [valor] and borne by their memory, let us continue to stand for the ideals for which they lived and died.

President Reagan appealed to the heritage of America's origins to convince a new generation to not let go of the courage or confidence in the value of liberty. He stressed that it is worth fighting for, that freedom is not only a worthy goal, but is also an attainable one, no matter how powerful tyrants seem to be. Our nation originated because many held to this basic faith, and our nation will flourish as many continue to hold onto this basic faith.

27

The States have no power, by taxation or otherwise, to retard, impede, burden, or in any manner control, the operations of the constitutional laws enacted by Congress to carry into execution the powers vested in the general government.
—CHIEF JUSTICE MARSHALL
ON BEHALF OF THE SUPREME COURT

Another landmark Supreme Court case, *McCulloch v. Maryland* came about because the state of Maryland imposed a tax on all bank notes from banks that were not chartered in Maryland. From the decision of the court, which ruled against the state of Maryland, the principle now stands that Congress has been granted implied powers by the Constitution in order to enact the express powers granted to it by the Constitution.

McCulloch v. Maryland, March 6, 1819

In the case now to be determined, the defendant, a sovereign State, denies the obligation of a law enacted by the legislature of the Union, and the plaintiff, on his part,

contests the validity of an act which has been passed by
the legislature of that State. The constitution of our country,
in its most interesting and vital parts, is to be considered;
the conflicting powers of the government of the Union and
of its members, as marked in that constitution, are to be
discussed; and an opinion given, which may essentially
influence the great operations of the government.

Precipitating this 1819 Supreme Court decision, Maryland passed
a law taxing the Second Bank of the United States, which was established by Congress in 1816. A branch of the U.S. Bank refused
to pay the Maryland tax. The Maryland Court of Appeals ruled
that the Maryland tax was valid because there was no authorization
in the Constitution for Congress to create a national bank. The
Supreme Court had to rule on whether or not a bank was constitutional and, if so, whether or not a state government's power to tax
extended to the operations of the federal government.

This great principle is, that the constitution and the laws
made in pursuance thereof are supreme; that they control
the constitution and laws of the respective States, and
cannot be controlled by them. From this, which may be
almost termed an axiom, other propositions are deduced
as corollaries, on the truth or error of which, and on their
application to this case, the cause has been supposed to
depend. These are, 1st. that a power to create implies a
power to preserve. 2nd. That a power to destroy, if wielded
by a different hand, is hostile to, and incompatible with
these powers to create and to preserve. 3d. That where this

repugnancy exists, that authority which is supreme must
control, not yield to that over which it is supreme. . . .

The legitimate actions of the federal government cannot be weak-
ened or blocked by state governments. It is impossible to have a
federal government carry out its constitutional functions if the
states can obstruct those functions.

...taxation is said to be an absolute power, which
acknowledges no other limits than those expressly
prescribed in the constitution, and like sovereign power of
every other description, is trusted to the discretion of those
who use it. But the very terms of this argument admit that
the sovereignty of the State, in the article of taxation itself,
is subordinate to, and may be controlled by, the constitution
of the United States. How far it has been controlled by that
instrument must be a question of construction.

Here, it is noted that the sovereign right of a state to impose taxes cannot be unlimited. The federal plan of the Constitution requires that
a state's authority to tax must be subject to the national government.

The argument on the part of the State of Maryland is, not
that the States may directly resist a law of Congress, but
that they may exercise their acknowledged powers upon
it, and that the constitution leaves them this right in the
confidence that they will not abuse it.

Maryland claimed that taxing the bank was not the same as refusing to allow the bank to operate. They were abiding by the law and keeping within their proper place. As a state, they had the power and right to raise revenue. Therefore, they reasoned, they could tax the national bank.

The sovereignty of a State extends to everything which exists by its own authority, or is so introduced by its permission; but does it extend to those means which are employed by Congress to carry into execution powers conferred on that body by the people of the United States? We think it demonstrable that it does not. Those powers are not given by the people of a single State. They are given by the people of the United States, to a government whose laws, made in pursuance of the constitution, are declared to be supreme. Consequently, the people of a single State cannot confer a sovereignty which will extend over them.

While "we the people" established the Constitution and the federal government, the people of the United States never established Maryland as a state able to tax that federal government. Maryland is a state for those living in Maryland, and it is not sovereign over all the people of the United States, therefore, it does not have the authority to tax the federal government.

The result is a conviction that the States have no power, by taxation or otherwise, to retard, impede, burden, or in any manner control, the operations of the constitutional laws enacted by Congress to carry into execution the powers

vested in the general government. This is, we think, the unavoidable consequence of that supremacy which the constitution has declared.

Notice that the Supreme Court understood that taxes are damaging to people—that the power to tax is a way to control people and their activities. That is why, according to the Supreme Court, it is inappropriate for a state to claim the power to tax an operation of the federal government.

28

> *I preach to you, then, my countrymen, that our country calls not for the life of ease but for the life of strenuous endeavor. If we stand idly by, if we seek merely swollen, slothful ease and ignoble peace, if we shrink from the hard contests where men must win at hazard of their lives and at the risk of all they hold dear, then the bolder and stronger peoples will pass us by, and will win for themselves the domination of the world.*
> —THEODORE ROOSEVELT

Theodore Roosevelt—soldier, hunter, explorer, author, and 26th President of the United States—was a sickly and weak child. As a result, he participated in several sports and physical activities to strengthen his body. These strenuous endeavors became a philosophy of life for Roosevelt, who believed that only a life full of activities, exertion, and striving was a life worth living. As president, his foreign policies were marked by the expression, "Speak softly and carry a big stick." Domestically, Roosevelt was a proponent of conservation, progressivism, and the increased regulation of businesses and monopolies. He is widely regarded as one of the best presidents in the history of America.

'The Strenuous Life,' by Theodore Roosevelt, April 11, 1899

In speaking to you, men of the greatest city of the West, men of the State which gave to the country Lincoln and Grant, men who preeminently and distinctly embody all that is most American in the American character I wish to preach, not the doctrine of ignoble ease, but the doctrine of the strenuous life. The life of toil and effort, of labor gold strife; to preach that highest form of success which comes, not to the man who desires mere easy peace, but to the man who does not shrink from danger, from hardship or from bitter toil, and who out of these wins the splendid ultimate triumph.

Roosevelt gave this speech in Chicago at a time when many in the nation were becoming concerned that American wealth and industrialism were causing people to grow soft. Like many others, he encouraged a practice of embracing toil and labor in order for individuals to achieve greatness for themselves and for the nation.

A life of slothful ease, a life of that peace which springs merely from lack either of desire or of power to strive after great things, is as little worthy of a nation as of an individual. I ask only that what every self-respecting American demands from himself and from his sons shall be demanded of the American nation as a whole. Who among you would teach

> your boys that ease, that peace, is to be the first Consideration
> in their eyes-to be the ultimate goal after which they strive?

When one is starving it is easy to get motivated to work and strive for a better life. But when people are satisfied with their basic needs, they can lose the motivation to pursue greater things. Roosevelt hoped Americans who had achieved a certain level of prosperity would set higher goals for themselves. In this way, America could become a great nation. Sloth and complacency on the part of its citizens spell doom for America.

> In the last analysis a healthy state can exist only when the
> men and women who make it up lead clean, vigorous,
> healthy lives; when the children are so trained that they shall
> endeavor, not to shirk difficulties, but to overcome them; not
> to seek ease, but to know how to wrest triumph from toil
> and risk. The man must be glad to do a man's work, to dare
> and endure and to labor; to keep himself, and to keep those
> dependent upon him. The woman must be the housewife, the
> helpmeet of the homemaker, the wise and fearless mother
> of many healthy children. In one of Daudet's powerful and
> melancholy books he speaks of "the fear of maternity, the
> haunting terror of the young wife of the present day." When
> such words can be truthfully written of a nation, that nation
> is rotten to the heart's core. When men fear work or fear
> righteous war, when women fear motherhood, they tremble
> on the brink of doom; and well it is that they should vanish
> from the earth, where they are fit subjects for the scorn of all

men and women who are themselves strong and brave and high-minded.

While the roles for men and women may seem old-fashioned, the basic work ethic Roosevelt described is a national requirement. John F. Kennedy later encouraged people in the same way to "ask not what you country can do for you, but ask what you can do for your country." The point is that people need to produce more than they consume, to contribute more than they take. A nation that fears to commit itself to work, defensive war, or children, will not last long. American greatness came from the courage to settle in an unknown land, go to war with Britain, and to tame the West. Without that courage, American greatness would not be what it was in 1899, nor will it last in the coming decades.

I preach to you, then, my countrymen, that our country calls not for the life of ease but for the life of strenuous endeavor. The twentieth century looms before us big with the fate of many nations. If we stand idly by, if we seek merely swollen, slothful ease and ignoble peace, if we shrink from the hard contests where men must win at hazard of their lives and at the risk of all they hold dear, then the bolder and stronger peoples will pass us by, and will win for themselves the domination of the world. Let us therefore boldly face the life of strife, resolute to do our duty well and manfully; resolute to uphold righteousness by deed and by word; resolute to be both honest and brave, to serve high ideals, yet to use practical methods. Above all, let us shrink from no strife,

moral or physical, within or without the nation, provided we are certain that the strife is justified, for it is only through strife, through hard and dangerous endeavor, that we shall ultimately win the goal of true national greatness.

Roosevelt's concluding sentence echoes the message of the apostle Paul in the Bible that "through many tribulations we must enter the kingdom of God" (Acts 14:22). He was confident that sacrifices would lead to a better life. He wanted people to possess a willingness to engage in physical labor with the understanding that such physical toil would build a character that was able to face hard moral choices and difficulties. According to Roosevelt, this character is not only critical for the individual, but it is also critical for the nation.

29

> *'Cast down your bucket where you are'—cast it down,*
> *making friends in every manly way of the people of*
> *all races by whom you are surrounded.*
> —BOOKER T. WASHINGTON

Booker T. Washington was born into slavery in 1856 to a white father and a slave mother in rural Virginia. After emancipation, he worked his way through college and eventually became a teacher. Later in life, Washington became a prominent African-American leader in the United States. His speech at the Atlanta Cotton States and International Exposition, before a predominantly white audience, gave him national recognition. This speech, which reflected Washington's philosophical belief that cooperation with whites was the best path to overcoming racism, is considered one of the most important in American history.

Booker T. Washington's Atlanta Compromise Speech, September 18, 1895

A ship lost at sea for many days suddenly sighted a friendly vessel. From the mast of the unfortunate vessel was seen a signal, "Water, water; we die of thirst!" The answer from the friendly vessel at once came back, "Cast down your bucket where you are." A second time the signal, "Water, send us water!" went up from the distressed vessel, and was answered, "Cast down your bucket where you are." A third and fourth signal for water was answered, "Cast down your bucket where you are." The captain of the distressed vessel, at last heeding the injunction, cast down his bucket, and it came up full of fresh, sparkling water from the mouth of the Amazon River.

To those of my race who depend on bettering their condition in a foreign land or who underestimate the importance of cultivating friendly relations with the Southern white man who is their next-door neighbor, I would say: "Cast down your bucket where you are" - cast it down, making friends in every manly way of the people of all races by whom you are surrounded.

Cast it down in agriculture, mechanics, in commerce, in domestic service, and in the professions. And in this connection it is well to bear in mind that whatever other sins the South may be called to bear, when it comes to business, pure and simple, it is in the South that the Negro is given a man's chance in the commercial world,

As Mr. Washington made clear in his introductory remarks, he wanted African-Americans to be optimistic about the prospects for bettering themselves in the South. Even though there was much injustice, there was also a great deal of opportunity. In fact, there were opportunities in the South that an African-American might not find up North. He suggested that Southern whites were more likely to employ and do business with African-Americans than their northern counterparts. By telling a dramatic vignette, Washington offered an illustration of the opportunity that existed for both whites and blacks right in their very community.

No race can prosper till it learns that there is as much dignity in tilling a field as in writing a poem. It is at the bottom of life we must begin, and not at the top. Nor should we permit our grievances to overshadow our opportunities.

It is easy to allow anger over poverty to blind a person to ways that could ease that poverty. Much like Roosevelt, who would preach about the strenuous life a few years later, Booker T. Washington wanted his fellow African-Americans to embrace work in order to achieve better economic circumstances.

To those of the white race who look to the incoming of those of foreign birth and strange tongue and habits for the prosperity of the South, were I permitted I would repeat what I have said to my own race, "Cast down your bucket where you are." Cast it down among the eight millions of Negroes whose habits you know, whose fidelity and love you have tested in days when to have proved treacherous meant the ruin of your firesides. Cast down your bucket among these people who have, without strikes and labor wars, tilled your fields, cleared your forests, built your railroads and cities, and brought forth treasures from the bowels of the earth, and helped to make possible this magnificent representation of the progress of the South. Casting down your bucket among my people, helping and encouraging them as you are doing on these grounds, and to education of head, hand, and heart, you will find that they will buy your surplus land, make blossom the waste places in your fields, and run your factories.

While doing this, you can be sure in the future, as in the past, that you and your families will be surrounded by the most patient, faithful, law-abiding, and unresentful people that the world has seen.

The exposition was aimed at attracting the interest of foreign markets, especially in Latin America. Washington wanted white Southerners to realize that another key to their prosperity lay in the labor force that lived with them in the same towns and counties. Just as African-Americans needed to be optimistic about working in the South, so white Southerners needed to be optimistic about African-Americans laboring in their midst.

No race that has anything to contribute to the markets of the world is long in any degree ostracized. It is important and right that all privileges of the law be ours, but it is vastly more important that we be prepared for the exercise of these privileges.

Washington wanted better treatment of African-Americans, but he believed that this would happen sooner if they worked at making a contribution to commerce and industry. In this way, their value to society would grow and they would be in a better position to win, and end, racial injustices.

... far above and beyond material benefits will be that higher good, that, let us pray God, will come, in a blotting out of sectional differences and racial animosities and suspicions, in a determination to administer absolute justice, in a willing obedience among all classes to the mandates of law.

This, coupled with our material prosperity, will bring into our beloved South a new heaven and a new earth.

Washington spent most of his speech describing the path to greater wealth for the South. But he made it clear that this was just a means to an end. His ultimate goal was real racial reconciliation. Like the signers of the Declaration of Independence, who asked for the protection of Providence, Mr. Washington hoped and prayed that God would transform the hearts of the people as they worked for one another.

30

Quotations about America

"The greatness of America lies not in being more enlightened than any other nation, but rather in her ability to repair her faults." —Alexis De Tocqueville, Democracy in America, Volume One, Chapter XIII

"Two things in America are astonishing: the changeableness of most human behavior and the strange stability of certain principles. Men are constantly on the move, but the spirit of humanity seems almost unmoved." –Alexis De Tocqueville, Democracy in America, Volume Two, Book Three, Chapter XXI

"No American will think it wrong of me if I proclaim that to have the United States at our side was to me the greatest joy. I could not fortell the course of events. I do not pretend to have measured accurately the martial might of Japan, but now at this very moment I knew the United States was in the war, up to the neck and in to the death. So we had won after all! ... Hitler's fate was sealed. Mussolini's fate was sealed. As for the Japanese, they would be ground to powder." —Winston Churchill, *The Second World War, Volume III: The Grand Alliance* (1950) Chapter 32 (Pearl Harbor)

★   ★   ★

"I should like to say first of all how much I have been impressed and encouraged by the breadth of view and sense of proportion which I have found in all quarters over here to which I have had access. Anyone who did not understand the size and solidarity of the foundations of the United States, might easily have expected to find an excited, disturbed, self-cantered atmosphere, with all minds fixed upon the novel, startling, and painful episodes of sudden war as they hit America. After all, the United States have been attacked and set upon by three most powerfully armed dictator states, the greatest military power in Europe, the greatest military power in Asia-Japan, Germany and Italy have all declared and are making war upon you, and the quarrel is opened which can only end in their overthrow or yours. But here in Washington in these memorable days I have found an Olympian fortitude which, far from being based upon complacency, is only the mask of an inflexible purpose and the proof of a sure, well-grounded confidence in the final outcome." –Winston Churchill, in his address before Congress, December 26, 1941

"Tell the world why you're proud of America. Tell them when the Star-Spangled Banner starts, Americans get to their feet, Hispanics, Irish, Italians, Central Europeans, East Europeans, Jews, Muslims, white, Asian, black, those who go back to the early settlers and those whose English is the same as some New York cab driver's I've dealt with... but whose sons and daughters could run for this Congress. Tell them why Americans, one and all, stand upright and respectful. Not because some state official told them to, but because whatever race, color, class or creed they are, being American means being free. That's why they're proud." — Tony Blair, Address to U.S. Congress, July 17, 2003

"Young man, there is America—which at this day serves for little more than to amuse you with stories of savage men and uncouth manners; yet shall, before you taste of death, show itself equal to the whole of that commerce which now attracts the envy of the world." –Edmund Burke, Second Speech on Conciliation with America, The Thirteen Resolutions, 1775

"I came here, where freedom is being defended, to serve it, and to live or die for it." —Casimir Pulaski, Polish immigrant who fought for American freedom in the Revolutionary War, in a letter to George Washington.

"America is still the land of opportunity. Mine is a universal story about how immigrants can succeed in this great country. That is our history. That is our heritage." –Ralph De La Vega, Cuban immigrant and CEO of AT&T Wireless (Poder360, November 2009).

"I'm in love with this country called America. I'm a huge fan of America, I'm one of those annoying fans, you know the ones that read the CD notes and follow you into bathrooms and ask you all kinds of annoying questions about why you didn't live up to that ... I'm that kind of fan. I read the Declaration of Independence and I've read the Constitution of the United States, and they are some liner notes, dude." —Bono, 2004 PENN Address

"America's abundance was created not by public sacrifices to the common good, but by the productive genius of free men who pursued their own personal interests and the making of their own private fortunes. They did not starve the people to pay for America's industrialization. They gave the people better jobs, higher wages, and cheaper goods with every new machine they invented, with every scientific discovery or technological advance – and thus the whole country was moving forward and profiting, not suffering, every step of the way." –Ayn Rand, *Capitalism: The Unknown Deal*

★   ★   ★

"Whoever is fortunate enough to be an American citizen came into the greatest inheritance man has ever enjoyed. He has had the benefit of every heroic and intellectual effort men have made for many thousands of years, realized at last. If Americans should now turn back, submit again to slavery, it would be a betrayal so base the human race might better perish." —Isabel Paterson, *The God of the Machine*, 1993

★   ★   ★

"There's a great deal of criticism about the United States, but there is one thing that nobody criticizes the United States for. Nobody thinks the United States went to strike against Iraq in order to gain land or water or oil, nobody thinks America has any ambitions about real estate. As it happened in the 20th century, the American boys went to fight in two world wars, many of them lost their lives. The United States won the wars, won the land, but you gave back every piece of it. America didn't keep anything out of her victories for herself. You gave back Japan, an improved Japan, you gave Germany, an improved Germany, you've heard the Marshall Plan. And today, I do not believe there is any serious person on earth who thinks the United States, whether you agree or don't agree with this strike, has any egoistic or material purposes in the war against Iraq. The reason is, for this strike, that you cannot let the world run wild. And people who are coming from different corners of our life, attack and kill women and children and innocent people, just out of the blue. And I think the whole world is lucky that there is a United States that has the will and the power to handle the new danger that has arrived on the 21st century." –Shimone Peres, October 20, 2004

Conclusion

Congratulations! You just spent the past thirty days with some of the greatest people who ever lived—America's Founding Fathers. As you read the Declaration of Independence, the Constitution, and the Bill of Rights, could you sense the destiny they must have felt, knowing they were paving the way for every generation of Americans who would follow them? When you read the Gettysburg Address, could you feel the passion surging through Lincoln's pen with his steadfast commitment to preserve our union? What about Martin Luther King, Jr.'s speech, "I Have a Dream," which he gave shortly before his assassination? As you read it, didn't his vision of a color-free society where every man and woman were free and equal cause your heart to stir?

America has been blessed with many far-sighted, noble leaders—men and women who committed their lives, their wealth, and their sacred honor to ensure that the freedoms we take for granted today would remain strong, unyielding, and intact. As you read the words of these leaders and felt their commitment, did you experience a sense of responsibility to preserve our American values for future generations? It's our foremost hope that you did.

Each time we read the inspiring documents of our American heritage, we understand our traditions a little better, a little more fully. We have a powerful birthright—an inheritance of freedom unequaled in world history. Truly, no nation has been more blessed than the United States of America. To preserve our freedoms, millions have fought for America—black, white, Asian, Native American, and Latino, many sacrificing their lives to ensure that we would remain free.

In the twenty-first century, our republic faces many challenges from without and within. The question is this: will we maintain our commitment to preserve our heritage, or will we be the generation that allows the American dream to become unrecognizable and slip away? As we see it, the stakes are this high, and the outcome is in doubt.

Sadly, millions have little knowledge of our heritage, of what our traditions really mean, and of what constitutes American values. They just float through life with little awareness of what has been required from others to make their lives carefree and easy. Voting for whoever will "guarantee" them prosperity, too many Americans lack the knowledge to make hard choices—choices that are informed and wise. By adopting the attitude of, "What's in it for me?" they forget President Kennedy's admonition to "ask not what your country can do for you, but what you can do for your country."

It's our hope that millions of our fellow citizens will read about our hallowed traditions and embrace the belief system of our great ancestors as their own. This is why we have written *We Believe*. And it's why we have focused on the original documents, giving you the opportunity to read them for yourself with little commentary. We are convinced that the words of our forefathers speak for themselves—that they have maintained their power over the centuries and will strengthen those who read them today with resolve and passion—just as they did when they were originally penned.

After spending the past month reading *We Believe*, has it impacted the way you think? Has it instilled in you a renewed sense of

duty? We certainly hope it has. Helping you understand the rich-
ness of our heritage is the primary reason we wrote the book.

Thomas Jefferson understood the importance of knowing our
heritage when he wrote:

> *Whenever the people are well informed, they can be trusted with*
> *their own government . . . . Whenever things get so far wrong as*
> *to attract their notice, they may be relied on to set them to rights.*

Jefferson believed that if people have a firm foundation in the
country's values and come to understand current issues, they will
take the right course of action—a course which honors our heritage—more often than not. This is our belief as well, and it's why
understanding our birthright is so important.

This is a time of great consequence in American history.
We stand at a crossroads with millions willing to desert our
American heritage to pursue an alternative direction. Not
knowing or understanding our birthright, they are willing to
abandon it. For those of us who do understand our birthright,
the need to stand firmly for what we believe in—just as our
forefathers did before us—has assumed greater importance.

Will you stand with us, strong and unafraid? Can America count on you to do what is right, regardless of whether
it benefits you or not? Will you put your nation first, before
your own interests—just as thousands of others have done
over the centuries?

George Santayana, the Spanish-American philosopher, essayist, and poet, once said, "Those who cannot remember the past are
condemned to repeat it." Will this be true of us? Will we wander so

far from our heritage that America will no longer be the land of the free or the home of the brave? Will this be our destiny, or will we once again rouse ourselves from our lethargy, shake the sleep from our eyes, and vigilantly stand for the great tradition we have inherited? Will the generations that follow us look to us as an example of strength and resolve, or will they point to us as the generation of weaklings who allowed it all to slip away?

Where you stand and what you do in the years to come will answer that question. Your actions—or your inactions—will determine the outcome. The choice is yours. What will you do?

We choose to stand in the great tradition that has preceded us, believing that no one can ever say it better than Patrick Henry did: "Give me liberty, or give me death."

—Jack Watts & David Dunham

Appendix

We hope you enjoyed reading what some prominent non-Americans had to say about our great country on Day 30. Here, we've included more great quotes, some from Americans and some not, some who were, or are, politicians, and others from the arts, business, and other professions. Many of these quotes are profound, and some are sobering, but all are intended to instruct and remind us of the greatness of our country and those core values that underpin her greatness.

"Let every nation know, whether it wishes us well or ill, that we shall pay any price, bear any burden, meet any hardship, support any friend, oppose any foe, to assure the survival and success of liberty."—President John F. Kennedy

"America will never be destroyed from the outside. If we falter and lose our freedoms, it will be because we destroyed ourselves."–President Abraham Lincoln

"You and I have a rendezvous with destiny. We will preserve for our children (America), the last best hope of man on earth, or we will sentence them to take the first step into a thousand years of darkness. If we fail, at least let our children and our children's children say of us we justified our brief moment here. We did all that could be done."—President Ronald W. Reagan

"Liberty is always unfinished business."—American Civil Liberties Union

"We trust Americans to recognize propaganda and misinformation, and to make their own decisions about what they read and believe."—American Library Association

"Equal rights for all, special privileges for none."—Thomas Jefferson, third American president and author of the Declaration of Independence

"Sure I wave the American flag. Do you know a better flag to wave? Sure I love my country with all her faults. I'm not ashamed of that, never have been, never will be." —John Wayne, American actor

"This nation will remain the land of the free only so long as it is the home of the brave."–Elmer Davis (1890-1958), American newspaperman, radio commentator, and author

"The American Revolution was a beginning, not a consummation."–President Woodrow Wilson

"This, then, is the state of the union: free and restless, growing and full of hope. So it was in the beginning. So it shall always be, while God is willing, and we are strong enough to keep the faith."—President Lyndon B. Johnson

"Those who expect to reap the blessings of freedom, must, like men, undergo the fatigue of supporting it."–Thomas Paine, English political writer, theorist, and activist

"Liberty is the breath of life to nations." — George Bernard Shaw, Irish playwright

"Patriotism is not short, frenzied outbursts of emotion, but the tranquil and steady dedication of a lifetime."–Adlai Stevenson, American politician

"Liberty means responsibility. That is why most men dread it."—George Bernard Shaw, *Man and Superman*, "Maxims: Liberty and Equality," (1905)

"The United States is the only country with a known birthday. All the rest began, they know not when, and grew into power, they know not how. If there had been no Independence Day, England and America combined would not be so great as each actually is. There is no "Republican," no "Democrat," on the Fourth of July—all are Americans. All feel that their country is greater than party."—James G. Blaine, U.S. representative (1830-1893)

"We must be free not because we claim freedom, but because we practice it."—William Faulkner, Nobel Prize-winning American author

★　　★　　★

"It does not require a majority to prevail, but rather an irate, tireless minority keen to set brush fires in people's minds."—Samuel Adams, Founding Father of America, statesman, and philosopher

"My God! How little do my countrymen know what precious blessings they are in possession of, and which no other people on earth enjoy!"—President Thomas Jefferson

"I'm proud to be an American, Where at least I know I'm free. I won't forget the men who died, who gave that right to me. I'll proudly stand up next to him to defend her still today, 'cuz there ain't no doubt I love this land. God bless the USA."–Lee Greenwood, American country music artist (from the song, "God Bless the USA")

"Posterity: you will never know how much it has cost my generation to preserve your freedom. I hope you will make good use of it."—President John Quincy Adams

"America is another name for opportunity. Our whole history appears like a last effort of divine providence on behalf of the human race."–Ralph Waldo Emerson, American philosopher, essayist, and poet

"There are those, I know, who will say that the liberation of humanity, the freedom of man and mind, is nothing but a dream. They are right. It is the American dream."
—Archibald MacLeish, American poet, writer, and the Librarian of Congress

"I believe in America because we have great dreams—and because we have the opportunity to make those dreams come true."—Wendell Wilkie, American businessman and politician

"At all times sincere friends of freedom have been rare, and its triumphs have been due to minorities. . ."—Lord Acton

"And that the said Constitution be never construed to authorize Congress to infringe the just liberty of the press, or the rights of conscience; or to prevent the people of the United States, who are peaceable citizens, from keeping their own arms; or to raise standing armies, unless necessary for the defense of the United States, or of some one or more of them; or to prevent the people from petitioning, in a peaceable and orderly manner, the federal legislature, for a redress of grievances; or to subject the people to unreasonable searches and seizures of their persons, papers or possessions."–Samuel Adams, Founding Father of America, statesman, and philosopher

"Freedom is the emancipation from the arbitrary rule of other men."—Mortimer Adler, American educator, philosopher, and author (1902-2001)

"Mankind is at its best when it is most free. This will be clear if we grasp the principle of liberty. We must recall that the basic principle is freedom of choice, which saying many have on their lips but few in their minds."–Dante, Italian poet (1265-1321)

"Better to starve free than be a fat slave."—Aesop (author of *Aesop's Fables*)

"Intellectual freedom is the right of every individual to both seek and receive information from all points of view without restriction. It provides for free access of all expressions of ideas through which any and all sides of a question, cause or movement may be explored."–American Library Association

★   ★   ★

"It will be of little avail to the people that the laws are made by men of their own choice, if the laws be so voluminous that they cannot be read, or so incoherent that they cannot be understood; if they be repealed or revised before they are promulgated, or undergo such incessant changes that no man who knows what the law is today can guess what it will be tomorrow."—Federalist No. 62, 1788

★   ★   ★

"Study history, study history. In history lies all the secrets of statecraft."—Winston Churchill

★   ★   ★

"The secret of happiness is freedom. The secret of freedom is courage. "–Thucydides

★   ★   ★

"We must not believe the many, who say that only free people ought to be educated, but we should rather believe the philosophers who say that only the educated are free."—Epictetus

★   ★   ★

"It has ever been my hobby-horse to see rising in America an empire of liberty, and a prospect of two or three hundred millions of freemen, without one noble or one king among them. You say it is impossible. If I should agree with you in this, I would still say, let us try the experiment, and preserve our equality as long as we can."–President John Adams

"America is a passionate idea or it is nothing. America is a human brotherhood or it is chaos."—Max Lerner, American author and journalist

"We dare not forget that we are the heirs of that first revolution."–President John F. Kennedy

"America will never be destroyed from the outside. If we falter and lose our freedoms, it will be because we destroyed ourselves."—President Abraham Lincoln

"The American Republic will endure until the day Congress discovers that it can bribe the public with the public's money."–Alexis de Tocqueville, French historian

*   *   *

"To live under the American Constitution is the greatest political privilege that was ever accorded to the human race."—President Calvin Coolidge

*   *   *

"Half of the American people have never read a newspaper. Half never voted for President. One hopes it is the same half."–Gore Vidal, American author

About the Authors

David Dunham

David Dunham is a veteran of book publishing; he has over three decades of experience in virtually every aspect of publishing, including acquisitions, editorial, packaging, sales, marketing, manufacturing, management, and literary representation. From 2002-2007, he served as Senior Vice President & Group Publisher for Thomas Nelson, Inc.—the sixth largest U.S. trade publisher. In this role, Dunham published twenty-five *New York Times* bestsellers.

In 2007, Dunham formed The Dunham Group, a publishing and entertainment agency specializing in management and brand building for its clients, which include artists, authors, actors, and entrepreneurs. The Dunham Group represents the intellectual properties of its clients through book publishing, television, film, licensing, product development, endorsements, web-based initiatives, and live events, and specializes in fresh approaches to product development, packaging, and marketing through multiple media platforms.

Jack Watts

Nearly all of Jack Watts' work for the past twenty-five years has been for Christian ministries and Christian publishers. In the last four years, Watts has spent more time writing than anything else.

His first book, *Hi, My Name Is Jack* (Winter 2012), is his story—a lifelong journey of recovery from alcoholism and familial dysfunction. Part of his journey involves religious abuse, which is why he has also written *Recovery from Religious Abuse: 11 Steps to Spiritual Freedom* (Winter 2011). Both books will be published by Howard Books, a division of Simon & Schuster.

In addition to these two book, Watts has written *Pushing Jesus* and will soon complete *365: One Day at a Time.*

Watts received an A.B. from Georgia State University in political science, an M.A. at Baylor University in church-state studies, and all but his dissertation for a Ph.D. at Emory University in international politics. He has been published in two scholarly journals.

Watts loves life and has lived it to the fullest, never opting for the easy way out. He has a great family, which has always been supportive. Watts lives in Atlanta and has for many years. In all he has five children and nine grandchildren. He's very active in their lives—it's who he is.